Sut McCaslin

◆

Sut McCaslin

◆

A Baseball Romance

Steve Spoerl

Writers Club Press
San Jose New York Lincoln Shanghai

Sut McCaslin
A Baseball Romance

Writers Club Press
an imprint of iUniverse.com, Inc.

For information address:
iUniverse.com, Inc.
620 North 48th Street
Suite 201
Lincoln, NE 68504-3467
www.iuniverse.com

ISBN: 0-595-13107-7

Printed in the United States of America

"The latest incarnation of Oedipus, the continued romance of Beauty and the Beast, stand this afternoon on the corner of Forty-second Street and Fifth Avenue, waiting for the traffic light to change."

Joseph Campbell,
The Hero with a Thousand Faces

"Let's play two!"

Ernie Banks

OPENING DAY

◆

Opening Day! Run! Wide deep green grass and stretching, run, the grass, the ballpark bounces, choppy waves on a green sea, bounces and run! All stretching and muscles stiff like I never used them and run! No games or rules just run! Crisp flannel uniform, spikes dig in the new earth then loose and run! Opening Day! Hot damn, the brand-new season and maybe this is the one, maybe this is the year, reach out and catch lightning in a bottle—

Running alone. Sut McCaslin chases after the team moving steadily away from him, across the ballpark. In the locker room Sut had knotted his shoelace and jerked at it, retying hurriedly and cursing as the team with one hopeful cheer ran out of the locker room. Sut came running after, too far behind to catch up.

Ted Williams smiles at him from behind a pack of Camels. The ballpark's old outfield fences are repainted this year with new ads and promises and topped with red-white-and-blue bunting for the game, Opening Day like a parade, every promise coming due and Sut runs, breathes deeply, smacks his chest with a fist and laughs, the big blue-on-red 'Senators' across his white uniform: Opening Day. Today is a holiday, flags fly in every corner of the ballpark. Looks nice. Sut smiles.

Sut turns, in center field deep in the ballpark. The team ahead of him wheels past the bullpen, flocking sharp starched white against all the green while Sut keeps pace, white dot on green, following after. A fan waves. Sut smiles and waves back.

Five years I've played in the Bigs and not started a hundred games but hey, the fans always remember. Once you make the team, scrub rookie or star, once you pull that uniform on, they all know you. I made the cut five years back and now I am a player, and next year, and the year after...

Damn I am an old ballplayer, he suddenly thinks. When they take down the flags and play the game. An old ballplayer in an old ballpark.

The team waits in the dugout. Ralph the manager hustles down the bench, pauses, points and shouts at a player. Sut plods on. The last fifty yards stretch out to a hundred. Hurry, hurry, says the chorus of fans, the game is beginning.

Sut runs on. Time was, back in smaller leagues, back after the war when I lead the Carolina League in runs batted in and they couldn't wait to call me up. Hey, you can bet they still remember old Sut down in Savannah. And before that, big-time in the army leagues and the low minors and back home in Iowa, on the state champ Legion teams and high school until I quit. Those days.

Sut is almost around the field. John Bunyan, the first baseman, stands in front of the visitor's dugout waiting for him. Sut slows, smiling. They jog across the infield to the home dugout. Ralph turns quickly and points to him. The game, thinks Sut. The ceremonies are under way and the game will soon begin.

Jeepers, it's the President. Sut smiles. Boyoboy, old Ike himself! Up there ready with the ball, beginning the new season all by himself, starting it off with that First Pitch. What a show. What on earth could match it? Every year it's the same, every year it's so new and exciting. The springtime air, the high blue skies, the green ballpark grass rolls out and away and the new season gushes in while the President and all the country watch!

Sut stands far to the rear, ballplayers from both teams spread before him in a deep semicircle around the President's box. Ike waves his arms and pounds his glove, so far away in the bright bunting as the crowd breaks like a wave over and around him, the smiling hungry gladhanders and the politicos, fat baseball execs, Ralph up there in the crowd too and the darksuited men sharp as razors clustered around Ike, these must be the secret service agents, guarding Ike, Ike Pater, Eisenhower my Eisenhower. The wind quickly flurries; Ike's nose is pink over his wide grin.

Now, just now, on this fresh spring day, the sky so high and blue, the grassed fields deep and wide, the promises all so true, Ike will start the season, rock gently back and deliver that first pitch. Sut taps his glove and waits for the throw. The President pounds his own, his motions so much larger and grander than Sut's. He bends slowly back and tosses the ball in a high, soft arc—the season has begun! Sut waits for the ball. No, it'll never get back this far. It has to.

Sut watches the ball float and thinks of an old-time newsreel, projected at just the wrong speed, everyone towering so huge on the screen and moving in their own time, the man speaking, turning slowly, the crowd about him in lugubrious exuberance—a hat floats into the air, a big fat bird of a hat meets its apex then drifts slowly down, down, recaptured by mundane gravity, not making the slow getaway—

It's over. The ball falls quickly, Seth Macy leaps and snaps it out of the air, pushes his way forward to the President to accept the ritual handshake and autograph. Sut understands. Every detail has its meaning. The President sits and the ballgame begins. Cleveland is in town.

The Indians pound them. A run in the first, five more in the second, three in the fifth, more and more runs. The man in the scoreboard pulls ropes for the runs, flips simple switches for the balls and strikes. Wooden slats clatter into place, small bulbs light the count. He adds two more runs to Cleveland's total and takes a cigaret break in the hallway. The President leaves.

"Christ, Keyser. Opening the damn season with a game like this." Ralph paces in the dugout. "We're too far behind to play for the win. Picking up eight-nine runs could be a week's work for this outfit, the way they looked in spring training. We can't even come back to look respectable."

"Put the bench in."

"We'll do that, Ed. See what the kids look like. This game is too far gone to try anything else. Maybe tomorrow."

At a bat a massive black Indian swings and drives the ball deep, deep, another few runs should score but Apollo far away in center times his leap perfectly, gloves the ball like a small miracle, a pure and useless act in a long-lost game.

"Cleveland's got the pennant fever this year, Ed. They come charging out of the blocks right at you. They're after more than just the paycheck." Ralph nods to himself. "And with the team we've got on the field—look at them, Ed. They're not even playing the same game. We have to get to them. It's the fundamentals. We have to move them, Ed."

Ed scratches his chin. He nods. He and Ralph understand each other perfectly. They began in baseball together, ages ago in the old Three-I League, later infielders together at Pittsburgh in the mid-twenties, traded and playing across the years until they both ended their active careers in Washington, a quiet backwater in baseball's wars. Ralph, a true student of the game, spent all his time on the bench, talking endless strategy and tactics with Bucky Harris, the old manager, running out to the bullpen to warm up every pitcher until Ralph knew pitching, playing all the positions on the diamond late in the games, learning and relearning the field, the game, the one story again and again, every detail of the story. Keyser played and listened. When Harris left, Ralph knew baseball and Keyser was his coach.

"And we'll have to make some changes in the field. I hate to do it, Ed, I want to keep the infield together but they just aren't working out. Put

Turle in at shortstop. But you do want to keep the same lineup, Ed. So the team will know each other and work together. You want the team to grow old together—that's how we did it, Ed. But it can't be done now, our players don't got it in them. McCaslin!" Ralph points down the bench. "Get yourself loose! Let's put you out in that pasture next inning and see what you got!"

Sut looks at Ralph and nods. All right. He wants to smile but he keeps a straight face. If you play on Opening Day there's nothing to keep you from playing every game, all season long. This could be the break, the one big move.

He pounds a pocket into his glove, leans back on the bench and surveys the field. He sits forward and reaches out of the dugout for a handful of dirt, rubs it into the pocket, shakes it out and looks closely at the glove.

Hardly been broken in at all. Just some fooling around on the farm and in spring training. Brand new this winter, hey, finally wore the old one out. The one Ralph made me buy. It took five good years, though. Lasted that long like some years I never used it. But a new glove, a new season, and next inning I'm going into the game.

On the field another of Cleveland's players, deft and certain, dives for the ball and cuts off the Senators' inning. The umpire barks yerout, disappointed baserunners wait for teammates to bring their gloves, Sut jumps and stretches. Off to the game! Things will change, this will be the year! Senators will catch fire, Sut will find the groove, the boon, bring home the bacon. He clatters up the wooden steps to the playing field. Ralph will call to the umpire, the p.a. will boom out his name, a buzzer sounding in the scoreboard will send his number rattling into the lineup, a wave of small applause and the President himself will write Sut's name on his scorecard.

Sut looks. The President is gone. Three outfielders race past Sut to their positions. Sut stops and watches.

"Hey Ralph," he calls. "Where did you want me to go?"

"Outfield," Ralph answers. "Out there. You're in for—for—" Ralph looks up and down the bench, then out to the three men in dirty white against the green. "Well, we'll get you out there next inning. I'll take Masaryk out. They fooled me that time, hustled themselves out there before I could get around to them changes." Ralph smiles. His glasses flash in the sun and his eyes disappear.

Right, Ralph. We'll go get them.

Cleveland scores, again and again. They drive the ball hard past Washington's leaping infielders and into the outfield among the three lonely men. The next man at bat takes aim and slaps the leather ball again.

Three long outs later the Senators retreat into the dugout, spikes click down the wooden steps, clack, clack against the cement floor. Bunyan drops on the bench beside Sut. He sweats in the cool air. John made two of the outs himself that inning, twisting like a trout to snatch a line shot from the air and later in the inning snaring a wild nervous throw from Macy at second.

"Where were you running off to with your glove, Sut? Going to skip over to the Clevelands? We can't have our rats running off the ship this early in the season, Sut."

"Hey, Ralph said he was going to put me in but I guess he lost count of the outfielders. Trying to add up the score and the ballclub both, he must of lost track. But he did say I would go in there later, get the chance to show off my glovework." Sut smiles, John laughs.

"You'd better remind him. He's probably forgotten already." Bunyan laughs again. "Come hot summer and things will settle down again. Ralph will drift off on the bench and leave Keyser to run the team."

"Hey! You McCaslin!" Ralph yells down the bench, stooped and pointing a finger. "Grab you a couple bats and get loose. You're up to bat for our friend Ramose this inning. The Cuban gentleman there is indisposed to swing for us." Ralph straightens up and smiles. He likes a good line.

Bunyan smiles, Sut shrugs. He reaches for a couple of bats and swings them slowly, heads out of the dugout for the on-deck circle. Pinch-hitting. Stand up and sit down, not out on the field, no running at all. If I do get on, they'll send in a pinch-runner. And then…O well, what the hell. That's the way the seasons go and I ought to be used to it by now. Opening Day.

"Did you want to go out in the field, Sut?" Ed Keyser stops him. "I'll tell Ralph, if that's what you want."

"No…" Sut pauses and looks at the diamond. Anything might happen. "No, I guess I'll just go up there quick and grab an early shower."

"All right." Keyser chuckles. "Maybe we can get you a starting shot when the A's come to town. They don't look to be doing much better than us."

Sut digs in at the plate. He sneers at the pitcher. He swings his bat, checks the plate and looks again at the pitcher. The pitcher sees nothing but the fat catcher's mitt. Let's be a hero. Two down. Slam a homer. Then we're only down by seven, eight runs. He looks down the baseline to Lock Graunt, the third base coach. Lock wipes his forehead, his chest, lifts and pulls his cap in elaborate mime.

Take it? Sut stares again. Take the pitch? Lock shrugs. Must be an order from Ralph, some whim. Makes no sense in the game. Sut shrugs and taps his bat against the plate, settles in.

The pitcher winds and fires and cuts the plate deadcenter. Sut takes strike one.

He swings the bat slowly as the catcher flips the ball back to his pitcher. Right there. I could have murdered it. Now this time I'm going. Won't even look at Lock. The hell with that. I'm up here to swing. Park the ball downtown.

Sut tenses. The pitcher smiles. He catches Sut's eye and there is the whole season ahead: games lost and long hot endless summer days and powerful Yankees and defeat, not tragedy but disappointment, despair, nothing. Sut swings. He only tops the ball, bounces it back to the pitcher on one easy hop. The pitcher picks up the ball, gently, takes it out of his glove and looks at it. He smiles again at Sut then strolls to the dugout. The team trots off the field too and the umpires amble toward each other. Sut stops halfway down the basepath.

Christ, aren't they even going to make a play on me? Sut jogs back to his dugout. Ralph jumps up, waving and shouting, redfaced and jumping and yelling.

"The batter is out," the first base umpire yells. "He left the basepath."

Sut staggers to a stop, looks at the umpire in pure amaze. Well, well, but everyone was leaving, doesn't that mean…Oh Christ, now I got to go back and listen to Ralph. Maybe I should have gone over to the Cleveland side.

"What are you doing, son! What are they passing out for brains these days! Damnitalltohellandback, McCaslin, you're farmed out to the Florida State League tomorrow! We need ballplayers here, not punch-and-judy—"

Keyser walks up behind Sut, pinches his elbow. "Better forget about starting for a while. Ralph won't calm down for a good week now." He winks and fades back into the dugout.

"Yeah, thanks. This will be the one thing Ralph carries to his grave."

Bunyan is doubled over laughing and the other Senators stare. Ralph screams. Sut wants to hide.

"All right! Let's get out on the field and back into the game! We can't just give up, not after a shit-head bone-head play like that! Get out there and put it to 'em!"

"Once more into the breach," Bunyan yells and leaps out of the dugout across the steps to the field.

"And for you, mister…" Ralph turns, looking for Sut, but Sut is long gone.

Hours past the ballgame Sut and John sit reflected in a huge mahogany-framed mirror, leaning over cold frosty beers, Sut nods at his reflection, he nods back, Bunyan studies his beer critically and tells Sut stories, over again, the same story with new moods and words and a surprise ending but no surprise because, says John, "Life is like that, and..."

Sut remembers too. He listens and stares into the mirror, Bunyan tells stories from the old days, about winning and losing, more games on this lost and lonely night without heroes, stories from the old seasons as they prepare for the new, Bunyan smiles and laughs and Sut stares into the mirror.

"But hell, after a while you get tired of all this pushing and scraping, all those numbers, always *having* to win. You miss what baseball is—"

The bright jukebox in the corner winds up, plaintive country wails drown him out. Bunyan clears his throat. "The game is the game. Hell." Bunyan turns on his stool. "Why do they bother keeping score, Sut?" They smile, a private joke, a last-place cellar team smile. "You ever wonder about that? They always know who wins in this league. And the cottonpickers here sure aren't going anyplace. They all know it. That should make life a whole lot easier, Sut. Why don't it?"

Sut peels a hardboiled egg. He salts it and takes half in one bite. "What are you complaining about? You're playing regular. Hey, you hit a double today, even scored a run. Congratulations, hero."

"Right. I take it." Bunyan smiles again. "We need all the heroes we can get. However they turn out." John smiles. In their game he *could* be a hero, transcend the game, become the game. He has thought of other lives, late at night over cold coffee and lighting another cigaret, wondering and waiting for the years after the game but today baseball is only a game, a round ball and a bat, surfaces meeting in sweet contact, everything easy and natural and nothing in the game he wouldn't expect. The long chorus calls Bunyan 'solid.' On the field he is never clumsy.

"Right, Sut," he says. "And I did have it. I used to have that pride, the drive, wanted to be the hero. But any more I prefer not to.

"I remember back when I was a rookie with Cleveland," says John. Sut listens. Another story, an old story, a true story. Sut will listen while Bunyan tells stories, or Macy or Ralph or the television or the whole world, Sut listens, he sits back and relaxes, folds his arms and leans on the table, pauses in outfield practice, shuts down his tractor to gaze across the wide fields and listens. Pictures flit through his mind, he smiles, the world's pleasures and secrets revealed to him and (in his mind's eye) gently transformed to the same setting, pastureland and American gothic imperium, all become the same story: A tapestry with one theme, one hero, the same journey past old boundaries.

"Hey, I remember," Bunyan says. Sut smiles.

"We had a great team that years, a sure bet for the pennant. I didn't get much playing time, only a kid, but I stayed on the bench all year and I learned. When you're gunning for the pennant, going for all the marbles, that's where you really see this game of baseball. It's not like this team, all you ever learn here is losing and forgetting and one man's highest average and the most numbers and maybe, maybe next year. That September salary drive. No, there with Cleveland we learned the team, how you covered for each other, made the sacrifice when the team needed it, poke the ball behind the runner even if it would cost you a hit, no, we all worked for the team win. A hell of a thing, Sut.

"That *was* a great team. Afraid of nothing. Pull a surprise bunt, delayed steal, the hit and run. Anything to get the ball moving, the fielders running, shake up the game. The people here, you'd think, would just as soon pop up, strike out, get it over with and out of the hot sun. Ought to install time clocks. Nothing happens, see, and the game don't change." Bunyan takes a long drink.

"Well, they had a victory parade for us at the last home stand. We closed out the season on the road, easy games with the Browns and A's. We were after the pennant, Sut! We had a small lead in the standings, only a couple games but we felt good, ahead of the pack. The Tigers and Yankees had to catch *us*.

"So after the last home game they drove us right through downtown Cleveland, from the ballpark to the train station. The whole town, damn near, was out cheering, throwing tickertape, all kinds of paper, it was just one hell of a mess. We had two players in each car, big new convertibles, sirens and police, just like we were off to war. Feller and Boudreau sat right up in the first car, a big old pearlgrey Caddy. I was toward the end, with the other rookie, Metcalfe.

"Opening Day—that's where it begins, Sut. And then the World Series. Anyone can get hot, make it, they say, but when you don't, you just say 'wait til next year.' And damn if we didn't finish just one game behind Detroit that year. Lost every single game on the road.

"And that next year, wouldn't you know it, the Yankees came back and blew everyone away. Took us by twenty-six games."

Bunyan smiles. It's a game, it's a liquid world, just shapes and forms and not one absolute among 'em, it's find out for yourself your strengths and limits, set your own standard, let them figure averages and percents to the last decimal but no, it's how the ball feels when it comes off your bat, arcs into the sky and that one brief unconscious instant, Bunyan plays the game and although he can't always explain to everyone, he adapts, finds his pace and lopes through baseball, it's like oil and water, he runs and watches his shadow move over the ground, silken on the grasstops, choppy across the scarred infield, greenblue and wavering under lights, around the bases, into home. Bunyan doesn't know baseball, he understands the game.

"Well hell, Sut, you've got to look at it this way, I've been in pro ball for ten or more seasons and I've got no scars to show for it," he laughs, Sut laughs, Sut has no scars either and last place is no place to find them. "Aw, and there's years ahead, Sut. Hey, I know a story," he says.

"And then there was the time..." John talks, Sut stares. The mirror across from him is huge, wall to wall, the glass flawless, their reflections sharp. The old ballplayers stare at him, no one new. Along the edges of the mirror photographs are taped to the glass or tucked in along the sides, quick captured moments and random views, newspaper clippings, cartoons and old dollar bills. The stories and headlines are from the local sports pages, legends and histories from the Senators' brighter days.

STEVENS PINS BROWNS, 2-1, CLINCHES PENNANT (every word a shout in fat thick letters but browned and flaky, a good twenty years old)

Wynn vs Chandler as Senators Vie for First

Harris and Vernon Lead Solons into New Season

And more ancient history. The latest clipping, the only one from the past five barren years, celebrates Sam Lear's no-hitter against the White Sox three seasons past. The newsprint is yellowed and faded.

Hooray for our team, says Sut. One time he really did believe all of this, honest and innocent, up from the minors at Savannah and breaking into the Big Show for the very first time, pinch-hitting and lining a double to left, Sut in the Major Leagues. That was the beginning, Washington the celestial city at the end of the journey. But it only began then. And every year the damn road is longer and longer and the only thing at the end of the road is, he sees, an end. But he comes back every year. Sut loves the game only playing, running across the field in mindless pleasure, chasing after a ball in flight.

The team is happy enough to see him return every spring, not because he is good but because he is trained. For these five years he has grown accustomed to his generation of players, their individual styles, actions and reactions, the stars and the scrubs all together in a tight world of gradual change. When his generation passes, as it will, Sut will become a fossil, a relic without familiars, past adaptation. Some day, he thinks, but until then I'm a Washington Senator.

"'Nats Bow to Powerful Tribe 12-2.' Nats, they call us. Like some damn insect." Bunyan reads from the evening paper. "They don't mention your play, though. Just give you a 0-for-1 in the box score. Guess they couldn't find the words for it."

"Words, hey. That's all it is, only them papers, nothing for us to worry about." Sut wants to be bitter, a cynic's clear vision, but romantic dreams of the game blind him. "Lose a game or two and they think we're done. But, hey, tomorrow we'll be back. We can do it." Why else do you play the game?

"Hey! Circle up, it's poker time!" Seth Macy, tiny and loud, slams open the screen door and struts in like a bantam, calls to everyone he sees, a shrill whine, a cackle. "Can't be wasting time," Macy shouts again, always moving, quick and nervous. "We got *cards* to get to!"

Zeke Hardy, the third baseman, follows Macy through the door. John and Sut get up and move over to a large round table. Two of Cleveland's ballplayers, inconspicuous and anonymous men out of uniform, grab chairs and join them.

"Let's see a fresh deck over here!" calls Macy and the bartender tosses a pack over the counter. Macy reaches and catches them in one hand and strips off the cellophane. "Hey, you throw just like that Ike feller." He pulls at a lump in his pocket. "Right there." Macy has the ball out, the ball Ike tossed to him. "Got to fix this up, varnish it or something." He sets it in the middle of the table.

"Are you putting that in the pot, Seth?" asks Bunyan.

Macy riffles, shuffles, slides the deck over to Hardy for the cut. "Don't be ridiculous, John. This is one of your American heirlooms. The first ball from Opening Day. Not something to be taken lightly. Now let's have those cards."

Seth deals. "Round and round," he calls, "ten, ace, spade deuce, king, king, nine. Check yourself and here we go." Nickels and quarters roll across the table, cards are gathered in and dealt out again all night long, another game for the players while in the center of the table the base-ball—'Best wishes, Ike'—beams at them, a smile in the looping stitches, a promise of things to come.

"How about it, Dale," Bunyan asks. "Are you people gonna beat the Yankees this year? Will anyone? Ever?"

"No, not with these cards. Well, we've got the horses, John. Look what we did to you today," he laughs. "But how many times running have those damn Yankees won? No one's beat them since we did back in '48. You remember that, John. You were on the team then. God, what a year that was."

"Yeah, you bet I remember. That was the year I got traded over here to Washington for pitching. I missed out on your World Serious."

"Oh. Yeah." He laughs. "Well, but if there's anyone going to beat them—"

"Nobody is," Macy says with authority. "And that's the hell of it, not just that those Yankees are so good, there's been good teams before come and gone. See, but the Yankees have what you call a *dynasty*. See? Check it in the *Sporting News*. Their minor league clubs, there's the key, the KC Blues, Richmond, Birmingham, they all win big down in those leagues too. The Yankees have a monopoly, see? They play it the American way. I'm telling you, those Yankees will be up there until we're all of us old men and we'll have to send our sons out to beat them. Damn!"

"Aw, Seth, teams have won before, teams'll win again. It's only baseball," says Bunyan. "Even the Senators were World Champions once."

"That's ancient history, John. This is about the right now and the game tomorrow. And the next ten or twenty years," says Macy. "It's all right there in the *Sporting News*, black and white, all the numbers laid out nice and neat. Statistics, they'll tell you." Macy waves. "Now give me a couple cards."

"Yeah, we'll find out soon enough who does belong up there. These fine springtime day games are one thing, but when the summer starts cooking and we're playing doubleheaders in Detroit, in St. Louis—"

"And those night games. Those damned night games."

"Oh yes. I tell you. I used to dream about playing baseball all my life when I was a kid. What could be better? But not those night games. No sir. I did not ever dream about playing night games."

"No shadows, shadows where you never expect them, the damnedest colors to things. That baseball looks like an aspireen tablet, bounces like a damn duck. No, lights and the nighttime was never meant for baseball."

"A lot of damn things never meant for baseball they're trying to push on us. Airplane rides. Television."

"Negroes," says Macy.

"And they talk about moving the teams around. Can you imagine that? We've had this fine baseball set-up for years, years now, and the Boston Braves want to up and move out to Omaha or Milwaukee somewhere."

"I tell you, not right."

"Baseball's the game, hey. It's all there. Why fool around with it?"

"Leave the game to the players, that's the ticket."

ON THE ROAD

◆

It's raining in Detroit. Sut can't think of a thing. He stares out his window. Late in the afternoon, dirty grey light in the sky, cars move slowly in the street and bleat, below Sut are long crawling lines of brand-new red, green and white cars honking, creeping, stopping and then a quick roar! through the slick streets, rubber sucking on concrete, wipers lashing and snarling, the horns bleat again for noise and tiny pedestrians lost in the wrong world scramble for safety. The ballgame washes away.

Hell of a deal, thinks Sut.

Dull thudding thunder, distant roars, machines howl below him. The day is grey, the sky concrete. Sut rises. The hotel room is small and clean, tight, deadly. He sits. Rain falls outside. He looks at the building across the street.

The Senators sit in seventh place. The season is well under way and the standings are much as predicted, Yankees breaking away from the pack, Indians and White Sox distantly challenging, the rest of the league bringing up the rear as the Senators play the Tigers.

A couple of wins, though...Maybe some other day.

The rain falls steadily, harder now, bounces high off the tin half-roof of the building opposite. The structure is solid, squat, empty. Windows boarded up over broken glass. An empty warehouse. Everything in Detroit looks like empty warehouses.

I could watch TV. Down in the lobby they have a set now. Free. He stretches. Hell of a way to begin a series, with a rainout. Bad sign. We could have won, too, maybe.

The tin roof is shaped like gentle waves. An alley cuts down the middle of the block and Sut can see old brick, unpainted. The front of the building is light green, flat industrial green, the color of a day in Detroit. Sut wants the building to shake and collapse, quickly, an unexplained earthquake, an augury for the future. Down the alley, painted on the old brick, he can make out an ancient advertisement, can barely read the faded words: "Bull Durham." The letters must be twenty feet high. On the street the lights change again and traffic roars. The great bull, faded and ghostlike, stalks the brick below its name. At the bottom Sut reads "The Old Reliable." Some paint from the front of the building has splattered over the neglected ad.

The season's gone. He leans out the window. Cold air, cold rain, a dozen games, twenty, fifty…Tomorrow they'll play two. Sut can wait.

A heavy truck passes below with a great grinding noise—and another right behind—and a third comes from the other direction. Sut feels the floor vibrate. He looks quickly across the street. Will it fall? He can see tiny chips of plaster flying—or rain? The trucks pass and the building survives, unmoved. Sut watches the rain.

Over the years Sut has become accustomed to waiting, timeless as a lizard, sitting by himself or with other silent ballplayers in beige hotel rooms skimming old *Popular Mechanics* or *Reader's Digests* over and over or just watching, staring straight ahead with no sense of anticipation but the schedule, a night game or a day game and then another game on the schedule, dealt out like a hand of cards and a beer, moving down the road to another city and waiting again, sitting looking out the window at unchanging cityscapes, an old man heading down the street going nowhere, Sut watches, waiting.

The rain turns slowly to hail. The wind whips quickly and cuts the air. People on the street huddle and curse, move slowly and run in spurts through cars and rain, Motor City. Sut watches. This must be how a plague begins. Little balls of ice falling, then bigger chunks, a whirlwind, then frogs and blood from out the sky—

Later, the rain stops.

Sut walks out of the hotel alone. He lights a cigaret and tosses the match away. He never smokes at home but Bunyan is paid to endorse these and gets free cartons. Sut draws the smoke in, looks both ways down the street. He lets the smoke out and follows the drift.

Old sad buildings slump together under the smudged sky, cars roar, wet newspapers stick to the filthy sidewalks. Taverns play rickety antique music, fleabag hotels wink blink neon on and off, Jesus Saves, on and off, men stagger by. Sut turns down a side street away from the traffic, past deserted truck docks and empty buildings. Weeds push through cracks in the sidewalks.

Sut bends and picks one. The first good sign I've seen, he thinks. Life somewhere in this city.

Back home on the farm he fights them, waging a natural battle, but here in the midst of the city he finds an ally. He breaks the weed, rubs it between his fingers, smells the green. Green, insistent, alive. Sut walks on down the street.

In Detroit the cars, the city and its buildings oppress him. After the rain oil and grease cling to every surface, drops stand out like rhinestones in the sun then trickle away down the sidewalks to sewers, back to the rivers and the oceans and next time in an endless cycle fall on the earth, the land, growth and renewal. He breathes in; oil and burnt gas fill his lungs, carbon settles on his clothes. City blocks border right on the streets, no front yards but narrow slimy walls, a dangerous tunnel and all those cars.

None of this at home. There, on his farm, Sut is both sower and reaper and sees more than you might imagine. Farming, that's the ticket, he always says to anyone who will listen. He wouldn't be out in the cities at all, ever, he tells himself, or even playing ball if it were not for the mortgages on his land. He always says that but come spring, every year, he is in Washington, playing.

Off the field, surrounded by the city, Sut feels lost. He stays inside playing cards with other ballplayers or by himself, at a hotel on the road or the small apartment he shares with Bunyan in DC. He keeps a window-garden there. He can't grow much but he feels better when he sees it there. He can lay in bed and watch the vines as they climb the stalks, fresh and live-green in the city. He's raising tomatoes.

He remembers when he built the window-box, a few days before the season began. Bunyan watched him bring in lumber and potting soil. "What are you doing, Sut? What in the hell are you bringing more dirt in here for? Don't we have enough already?"

"I'm making us a garden, boy. We'll have fresh tomatoes right out the window. Just lean out and pick 'em off the vine, right in the middle of the city."

"Just walk around the corner and buy some. Just leave all the dirt out of here. Just leave all them bugs go somewhere else. What *are* you doing?"

"A little initiative, John. I want to see something when I look out the window. Not smoke and buildings, something real, something that grows, see, useful. But not just flowers, nothing like that..."

Sut doesn't like flowers. They don't serve him any purpose, don't even help the soil like clover. They just grow, he says. Some of them do look all right, he has to admit that. Some of them have nice colors. But all the trouble Christiana goes through just for colors.

His wife has a garden on the farm. They had grown vegetables around the house for years, as far back as Sut could remember. First a small truck garden and then in the war a victory garden, proud cabbages and turnips holding a tertiary defense-line against fascism. But Sut wanted new land

and when he first made the majors, survived the final roster cut, he celebrated and took out a mortgage on the old farm south of his own.

The new land had a large and flourishing salad garden so he gave his wife the land around the house. He figured it to be almost dead and now he had new land to work. He spaded the earth for her, deeply, and forgot.

The garden bloomed. When he left for the start of his first big league season, the land was barren but looked promising, newly turned. He saw the flowers when he first returned in July at the All-Star break. Brilliant whites, reds, blues, here contrasting and there complementing, pastel and shocking shades, a rainbow in the ground around his house that astonished and for a time pleased him. He was surprised by the work she could put into the garden and still keep up with her share of the chores.

She came into the house on the second day, flushed and excited, skyblue eyes bright. She sat beside him and put her hand on his knee and talked. She had names for the flowers, she understood them. Sut listened for a while, then went back to his paper. At home he rested while his brothers farmed for him. Sut was in baseball from seedtime to harvest.

Sut understands where he is, his world is tangible and exact. Gentleman-farmer (he smiles) and 'Valuable reserve and pinch-hitter' as it says on the new bubblegum cards. Flowers cover his front yard, ivy and vines twine 'round his home. The crops and corn pay for themselves and almost every day his name is in the papers. Sut McCaslin is happy. He crumbles the weed, tosses it away and walks on down the street.

"Baseball," says Macy. "Not a damn thing on earth like it."

Bunyan shuffles a deck of crisp new cards, ruffles and stacks them carefully as he builds himself a house. Quickly, his hand is deft, he lays an elaborate foundation of nines and tens. Sut taps his glass to see the bubbles dance. Hardy watches. The bar is empty. Bunyan starts on his second tier. They sit under one dirty spotlight late at night.

"I was all fired up for the game today too," says Macy. "Looking for a real contest, a victory. We'll play two tomorrow, men. See, that's where the game is. Struggle, go for it and the best of the teams takes home the marbles. Play for the breaks, size up the other guy and go after him. Do it the American way.

"Now there's the Yankees, see? Today they won big again, up in Boston. Scored eight, nine runs. Can you imagine that? What that would be like, to be a Yankee? Now they *win* all the time. We make a damn good living playing ball in this country, but those guys, see, they're the best. The best now, maybe the best forever—" Macy drinks and dreams and finds his totem in the pages of *Baseball Digest*: '...the power of Ruth, the concentration of Ted Williams and the fierce drive of Cobb...' Seth imagines one monolithic creation, perfect myth, vindicating itself over and again in the flawless execution of its deeds, an iron will, an absolute fascist. It could walk into the bar at any moment.

Macy stares at the center of the table. His cigaret wiggles in his hand, he sits smoking and talking as he punctuates himself with short jabs and spins in constant small circles while he argues with himself. He comes to a conclusion, not a new one but one of the old realized again, takes a quick puff, leans back with his eyes closed and says "See?," waits a moment before he continues.

"It's a game that makes sense. You see that. There is absolutely nothing *confusing* about the game. You've got your rules, they tell you what to aim for. You know how far to go." The game in his mind, the game on the field, the organized and the organic: Seth holds the contradictions easily, rises above the intellect to his emotions. "Now you take the scoring in the game. The scores are valid. They're true. Games are like five to three, four to two."

"They've been two to ten and three to twelve lately," says Bunyan. He plays the game too, on the same field. Tonight the game is done. He shows Sut an ace, places it as a turret on his card house.

Macy waves his hand. "No, see, it's because you have to be good to make it all the way home. Nothing like in this basketball, where you get people scoring seventy, eighty points. What good is one point in all of that? Nothing. Same as football, there it's twenty, thirty points at a crack." He leans back and opens his arms. He waits.

"But in baseball. See? Now there a point means something. You score a run and people talk about you. They know you've accomplished something. You've got RBIs and you've got runs scored. Now look at this Enos Slaughter. People talk about him, he's good, but the one thing they *always* mention is that run, the one he scores all the way from first in the World Series.

"What a game. I'm telling you." Macy smokes again and jabs with his cigaret. "And it's not just what's in the rules. No siree. It's in how you throw the infield ball around, the way it goes around the horn, the pitcher's warmups and then the catcher throws down to second, perfect, see? Those all have to be just right and then, *only* then, do you start the next inning. That's the way it goes. You got to have all of that down pat before you can ever hope of making the Bigs.

"Those other games got none of it. You know what sport we was meant to play. Baseball, straight ahead. Think of some of the crazy things you do in those other sports. Take the rules and turn 'em. Pull dumb stunts like the Statue of Liberty or the Harlem Globetrotters. And then on top a that you go out and change the goals around halfway through the game. That's not right."

"But hell, Macy," says Bunyan, "in baseball where you score is where you start out from. How do you figure that?"

"What in hell is that supposed to mean, Bunyan? That is straight-out nonsense. Christ. And, well, there's boxing, see? Another sport they try to push off on you. Now there you're trying to kill somebody " Macy nudges the table. Bunyan's four floors of Bicycles come tumbling down.

"Hey. Seth, look what you did. The first thing I've done right all day and you have to knock it over." John winks at Sut.

"Sorry, sorry, didn't know it meant so damn much to you." Macy waves his hand, flips the ash from his cigaret. "Can't be fooling around all the time. There's things happening in this country you'd never suspect. But we still got the game.

"And the hell of it is," he settles back in his chair, "baseball used to be even greater. Back in the old days. Teddy Roosevelt was the president and we took no one's guff. In baseball, those old-time days, there were the great ones, the giants. Your game was a real tactical battle, this one-run-at-a-time game, you'd play for the single shot and hold it tight all the way. There was McGraw. Mordecai Brown. Mathewson. Cobb." The names roll off his tongue. He savors the memory, the stories handed down from years past.

"You'd bunt for a single, steal second, go to third on an infield out and then score on a long fly ball. Play the game, hold 'em. Someone that could pop that ball to right, control his bat, set up the game, how it's gonna go, wouldn't matter if your average was just one-fifty, see, if you knew the game, if you always hit behind the runner, advanced him, protected him on steals, see, play that inside game, well, that man was in the lineup. A man that can play. Doesn't matter what the numbers say, you needed the team man.

"If you went up there and swung for the fences, struck out all the time and hit into lollyass double plays, why, you weren't any kind of major leaguer. And now, modern times, seems like that's all we got in the lineups, them fence-busting showboats."

"A bunch of Babe Ruths."

"No!" Macy jumps. "Not a one of them is Babe Ruth! No, you're sad mistaken there! Babe Ruth *was* the game!" Macy waves his hands, conjures a vision only he can see. The bar is empty, a cosmos waiting to be filled. "Ruth comes along when the game was down, when they found gambling and fixed games and all, Ruth took his big swing and then and there changed the whole set-up. It takes a hero, see, it takes the biggest hero of all to *change* the game just like that, make the people forget all about the shameful Black Sox and the war just ended, no, Ruth stepped in and changed the game, the whole way a man plays." Macy isn't in the bar, he doesn't know where he is: a baseball Valhalla full of giants and Giants. His chair teeters, he grabs the table and awakens.

"Glad to see you're back among us, Seth. Thought we'd have to dip you in formaldehyde and stick you in a corner at Cooperstown," says Bunyan.

"Nothing funny, John," Macy says. "Nothing funny about it. Baseball's given you a damn good living and it behooves you to understand it. Part of our country, you know, a big part. It just means so much to everyone. Shows you something. The country is always watching and they know, they know. The man who wins is a hero. The man who never loses— there was Ruth, and that was it. Now it goes to show the American way. So what do they play in Russia? See? Who knows? But the Yankees play for the World Series.

"The rest of the world isn't up to snuff. Politicians. Movie stars. That's about it. Now who are you gonna pick, Babe Ruth or Mussolini?" Seth smiles, satisfied. He looks out the window. An idea like a specter stares at him.

"These foreign countries, all they've had is wars and revolutions, pot-shot dictators and hard times. No wonder they're a little confused about things. And communism creeping all over Europe. There's that Malenkov, you know him. Looks just like Jackie Gleason. Right now he's leading the conspiracy but you never know who's really on top. They don't have our peace, our great times, they don't have our great future, can't play our sports or nothing so they're out to bury us."

"Amen to that," says Hardy. "I been in one war already, but if it comes down to that, I'll go again."

Bunyan smiles. "Damn right, I would too. I remember the last one. Sat on an island in the Pacific for three years and played ball. Had a bunch of ballplayers from the draft there, they called us a supply depot. Every few weeks we'd go out on tour and play other company, division teams, then back to our island. Hey, we had first crack at the beer, after the sea bees. Cool 'em down with a can of bug spray and go out and play a few more innings. Hell, yes, I'd go to war again too."

"Nothing like that, John," says Macy. His voice is steel. "This is serious talk. Can't have no joking around." He spits. "Now we were there in Germany, where the real war was. I was with Patton, hey, you can bet we was ready to roll. Wouldn't have taken nothing to flatten them reds then. But now! Damn it, John, there is a world wide conspiracy now, in this country and all over the world, dedicated to plowing us under and you tell jokes! Look at the army! Look at the Hearings!"

"Aren't they on that TV about now?" says Hardy. "Seems it's about time for that highlights show. Damn, I wish I could watch the whole show in the daytime. When we start to play a few more night games, there's the key."

"The day's coming," says Macy.

Sut smiles. There is something in the air. Once he almost understood these Hearings, this McCarthy and the strange careers of men, could relate them to other stories, stories in the wind about traitors, the hope and the glory, o'er the ramparts and he knows, he was in the war too, off to fight after an older brother came back to the farm in '44. He knew his side would win, always wins, he was there crossing the Rhine (in a quartermaster's corps in late '45), but now in the late hours of the world they say that some on his side are actually on *their* side. He knew about old Benedict Arnold but hell, he says, that's just in the history books. But now there's that senator, in the newspapers and radio, Hardy turns on the TV set and there he is again, with tales of traitors and high intrigue, waving papers and pointing and shouting, feral, savage.

Sut looks at Macy. "But they're saying that in the Army, in the US Army there are card-carrying—"

"Naw, that's not what's important, look at it this way, Sut." Macy sits quickly forward. His eyes dart. He takes in the room. "You too, John. Get the true facts. Now it's not the ones with cards you have to worry about. You can always catch them. But, see, if all the Communists were card-carrying and registered. And if they all followed the party line. Then we would not have one bit of trouble. Rooting them out and getting rid." Macy pauses heavily on each phrase and then the words come cascading: "But it's the ones we don't have any proof on that are the most dangerous, sure you can see that."

Seth sits close and argues past argument that his *is* the case, he sees what you can't, he makes his point then cracks his knuckles one at a time, a lurid fleshy noise, rocks in his chair, grabs and pulls, but grabs with words only, words past any reason, settles himself into old moves and old patterns as he pleads his case.

"It goes against the grain of the way an American is. It is not natural for an American to be a traitor," Seth says. "No wonder these folks are confused, can't handle themselves, have to go and help the red Russians. These are sick people we're dealing with, Sut."

Wait a minute. There was a hook in there somewhere and he thinks he has found it. "Hey, but if you don't have the proof—"

"Don't need it," Macy says. He is calm and reasonable. Men could easily mistake him. But a fire lights, his eyes spark, his hands move quickly across the table. "A commie is a commie and they always show their spots, sooner or later. Watch everyone, keep a close eye on a man that's suspect. They're after us, Sut. Always remember that. They want what we've got. They want to destroy us, each one of us, plow us under and let the grain grow, it's not a thing you want to just sit back and discuss calmly, no, no…" Macy's voice is softer and softer and only his hands speak, wave softly, dance his cigaret. Hardy points to the television set.

McCarthy covers the screen. He licks his lips, blinks, wipes his hand over his face. The camera is fascinated with him. Other voices speak but the television watches McCarthy. He leans on his fist, scratches his forehead, rubs and plays with his eyebrow. McCarthy picks up a pencil, scratches his nose with the eraser. He drops the pencil and shrugs at a shrill voice off screen. He looks into the camera and brightens, beams and sits straight in his chair and smiles into the television. He pushes back his chair and quickly rises.

"A point of order, Mr Chairman. Mr Chairman, I must be allowed an important point of...Personal privilege."

Macy stares. Bunyan gathers in his cards and deals a slow solitaire hand. "I must not..." McCarthy grips them. His voice is theirs, they share the same ghosts and fears. "I must be allowed to answer this most vicious attack on—"

"Now they're out to get McCarthy too!" Macy stares into every corner of the bar. "Those damn commies won't stop at nothing." Macy's hands move, pat his hair, scratch and brush. He points at the screen and nods, then lights another cigaret. "Damn," he puffs.

"The people out there, Mr Chairman." McCarthy points to the camera and reaches out to millions of tiny blue screens. What is this man, Sut wonders. "*They* are our jury. They will be the ones to judge us—not on these abstract issues, no, not on these transparent charges and frauds, but on the *real* issues. The issues of importance. The people, our grand folk out there, they know of what we speak."

A code, or a story. McCarthy is the story, yet he is a man like a person you would know. When Sut thinks of McCarthy, in his mind he sees a solid angular black shape thrusting suddenly into white light. What things are happening?

"Mr. Chairman, I must be allowed to answer these charges. An important point of personal privilege. At issue here—" He drones, he cajoles, his voice is flat and nasal, the voice of a thousand neighbors, broad, insinuating and hypnotic, fatal, moving so easily through Sut's mind.

"There is no question. The floor is yours, Senator. Proceed."

"Thank you, Mr. Chairman, I am glad, I must repeat that I am grateful to be allowed to answer these treacherous lying! charges before our national television audience. The people, Mr. Chairman…"

The people watch. McCarthy spans the country, in bars, in homes, appliance-store windows, multiple McCarthys in stacked banks of televisions at Sears, stretching coast to coast, border to border, California and Maine tied by a fat black umbilical of wires and pulses, McCarthy smiles, McCarthy leers, McCarthy badgers a pale witness on the stand, Sut watches fascinated and a little bit afraid and there are forces at work, forces in the air, brute dynamos miles away, distant thunder, Sut watches closely and for one second McCarthy trembles too, the forces touch them all at once, a question pulses through them: Where has it gone, what we had—but did we ever have it? What we knew—but did we know it? What we did—all of it was right, true, the blameless impulse of an innocent—

He looks at us. Hold fast, he says. The world won't change. Hold fast to a favored view, a stereo-card from life, things remembered are the way things were, hold fast, we won the war, we won, why are we losing, the world is free and all of it ours and we treasure a photograph from the war, a photo of a brave lonely Russian planting the red flag on the smoking ruins of the Reichstag and all will come to earth, the war is over and we all of us are rich, our wartime industry overtime and precious combat pay fat in our wallets as we salute the new day, a smiling sun rises over the peaceful blue ocean, seabirds glide, beaks wide open, smiling, agape, man in his new spirit, we are that man, a smiling dream from before the war, there was no world, the boundaries of family and home were the boundaries of life, hold fast, hold fast, where did it go, a wicked age of machines and conspiracy and fear crawling out of a black hole like an insect you can't deny—

Hold fast. He is sad, he is confused for a moment, the eyebrows quiver but we all come quickly to him and the camera smiles at him again—

"I want to tell the American people that as long as I!" words crash in brutal syllables "in your faith I will continue!"

"Look at that! Look at that!" Macy rises from his chair, eyes bugged, louder and louder. On the screen the Senator is only six inches tall. His poetry is savage and concrete. "That's how you grab those reds! Go out and put it to 'em!"

"Seth." Bunyan has watched McCarthy too. He leans on the table and rubs his forehead. Whatever he could say—pictures on the screen, McCarthy himself, a world of shapes, ragged nighttime dreams, can't let it mean anything, Bunyan says, it's only light and shadows, black and white and blue, turn the knob and McCarthy will disappear, or it's men in roles, a dream, a dead myth under blazing white light, no, he says. "But you were in the army, Seth. So were all of us. There wasn't any commies around, nothing like that. How could they be taking over the army? Doesn't make sense."

"Hey John, I'll tell you. It don't make sense how they took over China or half a Europe or none of those. But you see that it happened. Fifty years ago there wasn't a thousand of those reds around and now there's a billion. Like cancer, see? They just take over a country—traitors, spies, they buy them out and the whole country just falls. Rotten. That easy. The reds infiltrate for years. I don't know how they get them over here, sneak them in on submarines or something. But they are here. They're all over, there's no denying that. Just take a look at Alger Hiss. He was right up there, all the way back to when Roosevelt sold us out at Malta."

"But they say Hiss was innocent—"

"He wasn't! He was guilty! That's as true as can be!" Macy barks, leans his chair back until the legs bend. He perches, totters, then eases slowly forward and settles the chair on the floor. "Guilty. Guilty, John." His voice is a low threat. "He was a yellow-bellied red spy and Christ there is two hundred and five of those card-carrying communist bastards in the damn government right now. Two hundred and five. Communists."

Communists, thinks Sut. Strange unusual foreign objects: what are they? Men without bodies, a name for something never there. A shape, Sut sees, a dream, a nightmare.

"They said eighty-one on the TV—"

"Hey, John. Hey now." In moments Macy is perfectly reasonable, lucid, at peace with himself. He grasps the facts and they please him. "Eighty communists or two hundred or a thousand. Even just one, John. But think a minute. Christ. These are *communists*!" His hands slowly dance, he sees terrible visions. "This isn't dog catchers on the take or slot machines or nothing, this is the biggest damn conspiracy in the history of the world! Jew bankers and integration and Russians, each and every one out to get us. The whole damn kit and caboodle, everything adds up. They're after us, John. They want what we've got.

"The way they *use* people—like machines. Sometimes the folks don't even know how they serve the red master—fellow travelers, we call 'em. See, they create a network, it's like a spider web and you never know. You just never know.

"You know the Army has commies and sympathizers and cover-ups. Look at that Peress. A genuine red dentist. And who promoted Peress? It was that Zwicker. Follow it up. Marshall from out of the Army gave away Europe to the Russians, gave away the part Roosevelt didn't get around to. You see where it all leads, right up to the top. Up to Stevens. He's the boss of the outfit, the Secretary of the Army. He protects them all. And now because he can't fight any other way, he's drafted Schine away from McCarthy and the Committee. That is the grade-a work of a traitor!

"These aren't real times. The things that are happening can't be real, there's no truth to any of it. All those people. What are they doing to us? Hiss is one of them. Stevens. They are the ones who are selling us out. The big shots from the east coast. The ones up there in the mansions, those know-it-all ivy leagues. They're the ones. Achason. Hiss. That Owens Lattimore, and he's the biggest red in the country. Those aren't the real people, not by a long shot. We've been sitting out here long enough, watching what's going on there with those snotnose bastards kowtowing and giving away piece after piece of America, we've been sitting out here in the woods and not doing a thing about it, but we've stopped that, John. We've stopped all of that crap and we sent Mister Joe McCarthy here to take care of that damn mess in Washington! Damn!

"The truth, John, the real truth is that our interests are nobody else's business. Our gain has to be someone's loss. If we lose, they win.

"John, it's us or them."

Macy looks around the table. He picks up a card.

"Christ, it's the American way, the American way, you know." He looks at Sut. His face melts. He asks "What went wrong?"

It's a beautiful day for baseball! A bright new morning, the games *will* be played today, nothing could be more natural. The smiling sun agrees, steams dew off the diamond, dries the basepaths to a fine dust. A light breeze gusts out of the ballpark. Nothing finer than a double-header today!

"Remember when you were a kid, Ed, you'd just toss a bat in the air and choose-up teams? Just play all afternoon? Now—" Ralph waves at the ballplayers, his team scattered across the diamond. Slow working men toss grass-stained balls back and forth, dressed in drab visiting greys, strangers and enemies come to do battle in a far city: "Property of Washington Senators" stenciled across each chest. "Are we doing better now or what, Ed?"

"Getting paid," says Keyser. "Too old to just play."

"One time we never would have said that, Ed. Any game, we had to be there." Ralph picks up a loose ball. He looks at Keyser and smiles, a smug smile, cocksure as James Cagney. "Those corner-lot pickup games, Ed, playing with the kids you'd known all your life, sunup to—"

"The fans expect," Keyser says, nodding at the field. "Didn't have no fans for the kid games."

"Right, Ed. Right as rain." Ralph hurries across the field, short and bandied, tall Keyser walking slowly by his side. The morning light is hard and pleasant, a reminder of past games, a promise. Across the field Detroit's ballplayers wear bright starchy white, a crisp Gothic 'D' worn like a shield, reversed white on black on the caps. Ralph points.

"What we could do with a team like that, Ed! They've got the horses, players like Kaline and Kuenn don't come no dime a dozen. If you could only wake them up, get them up, get them to come around. Gardiner can't handle them right, that's why they're stuck down in fifth. Down here with us when they should be chasing the Yankees. Look at those guys."

"We've got the Senators. There's worse teams."

"Yeah. Damn it, Ed, we've got a team here too! We've got some players. All we need is a little luck." Ralph smiles, he dreams. A new team could rise from ashes. "Bunyan, Smith, they can hit the ball. Apollo's steady, Hardy's solid, there's players there. Cut the deadwood, forget the last couple years. Get some excitement on the field."

"A good win today."

"That'll do it. After those Yankees cleaned us. They've got it, Ed. Yankees are World Champions from now 'til doomsday because they've got the players.

"But it's not just talent, Ed. People have that and they still lose. Look at these Tigers. It's the breaks, how you take advantage of the little things in the game, it's teamwork, you've got to click together out on that field. Understand each other. When the ball's hit you can't hesitate, you have to be on it, you got to react like a machine and react like a man. Anything can happen out there, Ed. You've got to believe that and I tell you it don't take all that much faith." Ralph points to different players. "We're getting us a team together, Ed. That's what counts in this game.

"Look at Cott there. Just a kid. You've got to have a good catcher, one who knows the whole diamond, every situation."

"He'll play. Learn or drown."

"Right, Ed. And anything can happen. Who knows, some day the kid might turn out. Maybe he's another Cochrane." Ralph smiles. "A young one."

Out on the diamond Lock Graunt tirelessly trains the fielders, pounds ball after ball to each position, not a miss, clean-hit balls, one bounce, two, quick spurts of dust and snapped up by the fielders, fired back across the diamond in unchanging patterns.

"One time we were all a lot younger," Ralph says.

Lock swings and the ball jumps across the infield, Macy drives off his toes, intense and honest, twists and chases and comes up empty handed. He shrugs and lines up again behind Turle.

"I knew his old man," Ralph says. "He was a ballplayer too."

Preparing for today's game they pause to consider the past, keeping to the nature of the game. Though the present game is of live and vital moment, in every instant of each game there exists a quiet place for reflection, slow realization, tales from the past. Even the high tension of the game is sedate; men pause before putting the ball in play, playing out a thousand possibilities from a hundred games one more time.

"Jeb Macy."

"Right, Ed. You knew him too. He was playing his last year with the Braves when we come up. Now Jeb was a hard man to figure. He retired that year. He just quit. Had the talent to go on playing for years but no drive. It was a sad thing to see, Ed. Graceful in the field, a linedrive hitter, had it all down pat but you'd never see him get worked up in a game. Played like a zombie, like baseball was work. Now Seth here has the drive…" Ralph waves vaguely. Ed laughs.

"Now *his* old man," Ralph says, "Seth's grandad, Mike Macy, there was a real fire-eater. He played pro ball years and years back, haw, last century." Ralph smiles. "That's a hell of a way to figure it, Ed. Last century.

"I remember he come to one of our games once, an exhibition game down in Atlanta. What a character! Handlebar mustache, long wavy hair, got a new story every minute. He ended up taking both ballclubs out, us and the Cubs, steaks, he buys us fat sizzling steaks in a bar he owned, rolls out kegs of beer, all the time old Mike sits perched on a stool and tells us all stories from his days, old King Kelly, 'Slide Kelly Slide,' Cap Anson, Spaulding the player. The old Baltimore Orioles.

"Those were sharp players, Ed. They knew every angle, lived and breathed the game. Wasn't nothing happening out there they didn't know all about. Mike was a player like that. If he'd stayed in the game, he could have been one of the great ones." Ralph shakes his head. "Yeah, a lot of players like that. Could have been. Hey, I remember him paying off the waiters with hundred-dollar bills. He was riding high then. Had a lot of money but it comes and goes."

Ralph stops, looks around the ballpark again. "We got things to attend to, Ed. Business before we play the game." They walk into the clubhouse. "Hey, the whole family was ballplayers, Ed. Now that's something." On the field Macy scoops the next ball cleanly, throws it sizzling to Bunyan, twack! into his mitt.

"That's how it should always be, Ed." The clubhouse walls are green-painted cinder block, rickety card tables and benches scattered through the room, disinfectant in the air. "I saw Ruth and I tell about him. Doesn't matter where I saw him, in a ballpark or playing in an open field somewhere. Mike or my pappy, they saw Mack, King Kelly play and that's how I know about them. Not newspaper stories or stats or books, no. The oldest ones, back when the game was invented, they didn't even have names. Just the—what they did.

"Who's going to know about us, Ed, come twenty or thirty years? And who should? No, just, I saw Ruth, the Yankees won every game, I saw DiMaggio and Mantle. Not Ed Keyser batting two-fiftysix in '27. No, just the game, Ed.

"You got your players on the field, two teams. Sit on the grass out of play and watch. One side's going to beat the other, it won't be easy, the rules of the game keep each game close. That's all, that's plenty, that's what we're looking for. If they knew—if they ever stopped to watch a game, a pickup sandlot game on the corner. Slow everything down. Take the damn numbers off the uniforms, forget all them funny numbers. Just keep the outs, the inning and the score."

Ralph wears the number one on his uniform but Keyser doesn't mention that. "A couple wins here could be the break," he says. "Lear looked good last time out."

"That's right, Ed."

At the far end of the room Ralph has his office, a cubicle with a frosted-glass door. Inside on the wall he mounts a chart of the season, an oversize calendar of the baseball year. He marks each game-day with a large red 'W' or 'L.' Ralph brings the chart with him to each different ballpark.

"We've got a job to do, Ed. Got to get the players into the game." He points to the chart. Three big 'L's for the last three games. "Coming off those games in New York., we've got to give the players a talk. There's the ticket. Fire 'em up for the doubleheader. After those damned Yankees pounded us. But we'll come back. We'll give them something."

Gilly Jungfrau, low man on Gardiner's coaching staff, stops in the dugout before his team takes the field to warm up. The Tigers, a restless pack, swarm in front of their bench. Gilly stands on the Senators' dugout steps.

"Great days, you know, the sky clears up nice for us and you don't see it so high like today all that often, outfielders are gonna be a bunch of dizzy bastards today! How's it going, Ralph, Ed, hey I see the Yankees got to you these last few games. They are rough! No good to be in a series like that, it takes all your pitching, eats them right up. That will happen. That's right, Ralph, in fact I see that since Slade cooled them off in our opener we haven't beat them neither. But that's how it goes, I guess, I guess, that's why they're on top and we're down here fighting over the bones. That hitting, that power they have. They do have it! I see that they scored fourteen, was it fifteen runs off you that one game. Saturday, I think it was. Lucky us, we were playing the A's that day.

"But. Hey, what I did come over to see about—hey, and those White Sox is something too, this year. I never could see that Fox, myself, but he does one whale of a job. And Minoso! What we wouldn't give for him! They won't catch the big boys but they'll give you a fight all the way! Say, what happened was, we plain ran out. After the last A's game—Slade beats them too! He's really coming on this year, I think he's got the record! One damn fine game. I don't know if we plan to use him against you folks or not. Got a lot of fine pitchers this year!"

Ralph makes a small motion; Ed coughs and drops a baseball.

"But, hey, what happened was we damn just ran out of baseballs! Not but half a dozen to our good name, we can't even get loose properly! Can you imagine that! A ball club without any baseballs! Isn't that just the damnedest thing!" Gilly smiles and winks at both of them. "Fans will be coming in soon and they won't know what to think! The club-house man miscounted, had Slade, Dropo, Kaline signing up a bushel basket full, using up our good baseballs for souvenirs. And now we have us two games to play!"

Gilly shakes his head. The Tigers all watch Ralph anxiously, waiting for the game. "We sent out but nothing's come back yet. I say if that front office don't run us and organize us any better than *this*, something's got to pop! The boys we got, the players, they're all fine but they have got to get it together in that office.

"So we figure, three or four dozen. You know? That would last the game and give us some extra for warmups. Soon as ours come in, we'll pay you back, be sure of that!" Gilly smiles and jabs Ralph lightly on the shoulder. In the winter he sells insurance, successfully. He calls it 'assurance.' "Hey, they'd have us throwing gravel, dirt clods, wrapping up tape and bandages like little jigger-boys uptown, hey, think about *not* giving Jack Slade a baseball!"

Ralph waves to Ed. "Grab up a couple-three dozen extra, we got poor relations across the sea. Hand them over and see if them Tigers treat us any better today, playing us against our own damn balls."

"Well…Thanks!" Gilly takes the balls eagerly and waves the boxes over his head as he runs back across the field. The Tigers hurry onto the diamond and the early fans applaud.

"That's not right, Ed," Ralph says. "They're in the business themselves, they shouldn't come begging. But it's more than that."

"Gardiner didn't come asking," Keyser says.

"I didn't expect that. I sure wouldn't a gone over there begging. I'd send you or Lock. That's only right. But, Ed. They're going to beat us. Shit, with our own damn balls. Not right, Ed."

"If we win these!" Ralph jumps on a chair and waves his scorecard. "Sweep the Tigers today! Roll 'em back! Get rolling, men, team, we're on the move!" Ralph leaps! "The Brownies is sitting still and the A's is no place, the Tigers we're going to beat, get us a little steam up and it's look out New Yorkers! Team!"

"Go get 'em!" the ballplayers answer. Moments before game time they huddle in the locker room.

"Bunyan! Smith! We're out to stomp some ass! Swing those bats!"

Ballplayers in the bright sunfilled room mime their motions: Bunyan connects with a fantasy pitch and sends the ball deep, deep.

"Hardy! You're at third! Lear! On the mound!" Ralph points at each of them, bestows their task, an anointment. "McCannon! The batterymate!"

They rush together, bullpen, bench, starting crew. Soon they will take the field and anything might happen.

"Masaryk! Do us proud in right field! Because today, gentlemen—"

"Today!"

"Tigers! Tigers! We're the Washington Senators!" Ralph bounces high on the wooden chair and wins the ballgame for them. Keyser and Lock Graunt, arms folded like Turks, stand guard beside him. "Right! Right! Two games today and a game tomorrow and a game after that! Sweep the Tigers! We'll bounce ourselves right back from those damn Yankees and put a little fire in the belly of this league!" Ralph jumps—they run for the diamond. Game time, umpires, fans and Tigers awaiting.

Ralph hurries to home plate. The stands are thick, movement everywhere, an excited and noisy weekend crowd, ballpark full, bulky aging bull-like men in wildcolored sports shirts with their own stories—"I coulda been out there," nodding at the diamond, "They was gonna give me a tryout but"—and young boys running and old men, serious, perhaps this one once was a ballplayer too, closely watching the small action on the field and waiting for the game to begin. Ralph reaches across the plate and shakes hands with Gardiner, the Tiger manager, and Harvey Kuenn, the team captain. The umpire points to the corners of the field, explains the ground rules quickly and softly and exchanges the lineups. Ralph walks back to the dugout and the game begins.

The Tigers take the field and retire Washington in order.

Fat McCannon ambles across the field. Years ago he belonged here, a true pro, played every game behind the plate, every inning for weeks and weeks like an iron man, stood in at the plate in the heat of pennant races, toe-to-toe with the finest, young and strong and a flat belly. One day coming he can see himself sitting feet-up in the dugout, analyzing the game, calling out players' names and positions and that small part of their destiny, manage a team from his years of experience, but right now he is neither, a neuter, bullpen catcher and deep backup player, sitting in the far corner of the stadium counting balls and warming up pitchers, a fourth hand at pinochle with the coaches, put in the game only in the gravest emergency. Today the regular catcher is hurt, out for a week, and Cott the kid is starting the second game. McCannon has to play.

He squats behind the plate carefully, grimacing more painfully than he needs. The other players must know his sacrifices. The pitcher smirks at him and begins to throw, quick darting pitches straight across the plate. Come game time they'll jam those right back down your throat, bud. McCannon smiles.

"One more," the umpire says. "Game coming."

McCannon nods. "Coming down," he calls and the pitcher nods, McCannon checks the field quickly as he has done ten thousand innings before, the shortstop in midstride rolls the warmup ball to the dugout, the pitcher cocks his wrist toward the plate and McCannon nods, takes it all in, the sun and the sky and the wind, the diamond, shortstop trots behind second, the pitcher throws one last looping curve and the catcher leaps, here comes the game, old fat pro jumps and fires the ball hard, a little high, second baseman pulls the ball in and in pantomime motion sweeps across the bag where the runner would be…

The ball's a little high, Macy stretches, out of position with the tag (and the sliding runner will kick short and expertly, the ball pops! from Macy's glove and rolls slowly away) across the bag and he tosses the ball to short, short fires to first, around the horn every inning, beginning the inning, John throws the ball high and lazy to third, Hardy snags it and flips it.out to the mound, 'Let's go get 'em now,' and the batter digs in, pitcher winds and delivers, batter cuts—

Macy pushes off the grass, measures the ball, cuts sharply to his left, grabs and gloves the ball bouncing on the run, halfsteps and fires to first, he runs, now screaming and waving his arms as the umpire spreads his arms wide, safe, Macy runs right up to the umpire and screams in his face. The umpire is calm and the runner remains safe.

"All right, all right, let's go get 'em." Ralph paces in the dugout, claps his hands and yells. "Don't mind them umps, they can't rob the whole game from us. We'll come right back, buck up, let's go," he calls. "Shit," he says.

Macy bends over, pounds his glove, waits for the next pitch. The runner leans. Macy leans. They are unforgivable enemies. Seth demands revenge. Spike him when he comes in, fall on him when he slides. Because he's trying to take me out too. Get him—

Macy makes the noises but when the time comes he holds back, can't play true gut level, can't play evil on the field, not a Cobb (Satan on spikes, a touch of violence, a spark of dark beauty playing against grace and harmony in the physical game), only poor. Seth can never accept his limitations, never really adapt to the far side of baseball morality, cannot bare himself thus shamelessly: he stops short, guilty, only guilty because he thinks he is.

Bruno John Petrarkis bats in the third. He swings at the first pitch, tries to check himself but taps the ball unexpectedly on a short hop back to the pitcher. Zuverink on the mound takes the ball like a gift and tosses lightly to first…Short. The ball drops, unexplained, an error, a break, a small tear in the fabric of the game.

"Let's go!" Ralph is up and pacing. "This is what we're looking for! The break! This is the big one!" His hands are alive, dancing across his uniform, lifting his cap, talking to the runner in baseball code. On the pitch Petrarkis is off, digging for his stolen base.

When Petrakis is back in the dugout, when (as he sees it) he has grabbed for the golden ring and come up short, had the chance and blew it, he must explain. Ceaseless, restless, pulling at a thread or tugging his ear, there is a reason for what went wrong, he says, facts that will explain him, proof past the fact of the ball in the fielder's glove. He paces and wonders. He has a catalog of errors and an index of understanding.

"Had him beat, Sut. A jump like I had should *always* beat the throw." Petrarkis the Speedy, the Iron Poodle. "But that throw! Like from a machine, you know? Right there, on the money. Right in the glove. I was out, Sut, but you have to admire a play like that."

Petrarkis has to admire what he can't touch. Nervous, he explains himself, over and again. From where he stands, none of his actions are valid without reflection, discussion between himself and his imagined audience.

"I tell you, Sut, it's a darn good thing all the league's catchers don't have that arm or I'd a be flat out of business. You have to admire the man."

Petrarkis sits on the bench. He explains. Otherwise he might seem more base or less well intentioned than he *knows* he was. And he knows. He knows what he means.

"But," he sputters, "but when the breaks start coming our way, then we'll show them, they'll see what we can do. Nothing we can do now but play, play the game and see how it goes. Free will," he explains. Petrarkis complains but he is happy on a loser, no doubts but self doubt, no pressure, no consequence to his decisions.

"The old batting average is dipping, but we'll get it back up. Ralph gives us a couple more starts and darn if I won't show them. Right?"

Sut nods.

"A game this close, no score, you've got to give it all you've got. For the team, you know. The better your average is, the more bases you steal, that's where your value to the team is, Sut. And they sure give us the chance that inning, Zuv don't throw all that many balls away, I should have been able to come all the way around after that play. If I made it into second, Sut, just a little base hit up the middle and we could have…"

Sut nods.

Bunyan strides up to the plate. He kicks the dirt, settles in, takes the first pitch and slams the next, the ball shoots alive across and through the infield and past the scrambling outfielder, Bunyan hurries down the line, turns past first head down and digging, slows and stops at second with a stand-up double.

"Attaboy, attaboy, attaboy!" Ralph couldn't be more excited if he had done it himself. He waves at Masaryk. "Hey you! C'mere!"

Masaryk, strolling to the plate, stops and turns back to Ralph. Masaryk is big, strong and chubby, a battered yet cherubic Slavic slugger. Ralph runs out of the dugout. Masaryk stands like a tree, massive.

His bat is a huge limb. He watches the stands while Ralph babbles to the sky.

"I want you to slam one out there!" Ralph points and the bleachers scream.

Masaryk twirls the bat over his head. "OK," he says.

Ralph runs toward the diamond. He yells at the pitcher. "Hey boy now! He's gonna slam one! We got you Tigers rolling both ways from Friday now!"

Ralph runs back to the dugout and Masaryk stands at the plate. The pitcher twirls and the batter swings, crack!flush he slams the ball and the fielders, both dugouts, the fans and the lonely pitcher, all watch the ball as smaller and smaller it floats away. The stands are silent. The ball lands without a sound high in the upper deck. Masaryk trots slowly around the bases. The Tigers ignore him but the Senators mob him, they go wild, hey, 2-0, hey hey we're going, we're on the way, a wild crazy formless feeling runs down the bench like electricity and maybe, just maybe—

Macy jumps and shouts. "We was jinxed at home! We're on the road, on the go now and we're gonna do it! Hey, this is a team! Damn, and here we go!" Ralph and the team are prancing and dancing, Senators off to that quick early lead and Lear's pitching, the best they've got, he's hanging tough today, hey!hey! and yes, maybe today—

Macy runs to the plate. His bat is small, barely more than a Little Leaguer's, ('Got to be able to control your stick,' he says) and each pitch is deadly fast and past him, he stands watching and can't believe the ball is so fast, that's not right, he wants to be a hero too. The next batter pops up and the Tigers come in from the field.

Lear takes the mound. The fat man is on fire. Seven years he has pitched for these Senators and he knows how rare, how fine and brief these early leads can be. But today he knows the Tigers are his, pitching from main strength he knows them intimately and brutally, pitching from the game's knowledge he retires batter after batter on high flies, slow skidding grounders, futile swings and lazy pops.

Lear thinks of himself, often. The only pitcher on a team without pitchers, resigned but ever dreaming, his thoughts are usually in the third person as he imagines fine stories for himself: 'Lear, the crafty young veteran, he has been around and he has a real future in this game.'

Once he imagined there would be a game, one for all time, he against the Yankees, playing in the Stadium. All things ride on the game, pennants and championships, future glories. Lear pitches from strength and knowledge, pitches with a great burden, heroic like no man they'd ever seen before. The game is tight, tense, animal. Lear takes them into the ninth, the Yankee home ninth, a hot and merciless place. Lear leads the game one-to-nothing. He retires two mighty Yankees, one to go, Lear sweating, valiant, straddling the mound hands on hips, proud and confident, waiting for the next batter, the last, a pinch-hitter.

Stengel rubs his hands. He looks down the bench, looks deep into the shadows. He points. Lear watches. What he sees—he looks again, watches the next batter swagger out of the dugout, pause in the on-deck circle, huge, swinging a handful of giant bats. A baseball animal. Lear stares fascinated. A golden aura, can't be helped, that's what he sees. A monumental man, a bull, another Yankee bull—*the* Yankee bull. Raw, wide, a fierce monstrous friendly face, he steps back and takes another slashing practice swing; the Bambino, the Sultan, the...The things they called him. Lear has two out in the ninth and he faces The Babe.

Lear wins these games. Games in his mind he can always cut the corners of the plate, break the curve off dramatically from the batter's shoulder to his knee, pitch with a strong heart and a willing mind, stay with the game until the end.

On the field he is a good ballplayer. He wins as much as he loses, sometimes more, is fooled less often than he might be, a no better than good ballplayer on a bad ballclub. Long chorus watches him and mutters, now if he were on a winner, what could he be...

Lear smiles. That'll be the day. The idea is good but he knows himself, he knows how it would go, Lear would pitch well, even brilliantly at times and keep his club up there but in the last days of the season, when the contenders are at each other in September and ballgames end in dusk and cool breezes, Lear would fold gracefully, curl like an autumn leaf and drift with his team to second place, third, after the last galling game of the season one voice in the dingy locker room says 'Wait 'til next year' and Lear smiles, he would say it too but not out loud.

"He's good, Ed. Got to admit that. Goddamn it." Ralph watches Lear loosening up, throwing to Lock Graunt before the inning starts. Two-oh, the game stays, into the eighth. Ralph leans against the bat racks and kicks a loose ball. They watch it roll. McCannon sits on the bench and pulls on his chest protector, adjusts the shinguards, tightens and loosens his mask.

"The tools of ignorance, McCannon," says Ralph. "We pick the players special who wear those." He looks at Keyser. "Lear's got to pitch the game out. There's the shits, Ed, nothing we can do about it."

Sut claps. "All right," he calls. He leans back on the bench. The inning starts, another inning on the bench, 'Best seat in the house,' he can tell his friends but even that isn't true. Sometimes he pinch-hits, plays a little in the field, late, but usually just sits and waits, watching the game and listening. It will all break down. It'll collapse. The thought hits him suddenly, blindly. All the energy's in one direction, a sequence that never changes, no drive, no tension…The idea fades away. What was that? he wonders briefly. He watches the game. Wouldn't it be something if just one day…

Crack! Another one goes deep! The Tigers come back into the game with a long home run. Sut sits up. Two batters poke singles, and Lear, now shaky, walks the next. Bases loaded in the bottom of the eighth!

Ralph calls time and makes the slow walk to the mound, out to hook Lear. The man's been good but the game is getting to him, that's what we've got a bullpen for. A few bad breaks can rattle anyone. That's how it is. Got to pull him. Stand out there, put out my hand and just give me the ball, mister, lay it down like an egg and hit the showers. Because you're done. Tight and serious.

Out in the bullpen Julio Ramose burns the ball, warms up fearlessly. The ball pop, pop, pops into the catcher's mitt. He'll pitch to anyone, anytime, not always so gracefully or effectively, but always ready.

On the mound Lear stretches and throws the ball half-speed at Ralph.

That's it, bud. O-kay, get the hell out of here because Lear is pitching this game. If we lose, it will be Lear that loses.

Ralph ducks, looks at Lear and hurries back to the dugout. The fans applaud, slow and confused. Ramose laughs and sits down. A new batter is at the plate.

All the same to Lear, Lear says in his mind. Lear is in control. Lear runs the game. Lear grips the new leather on the ball, holds it tight behind his back and watches the catcher's signals. Because this game is *over*. All right. This is it. Little fly to short right. One down. Forget the runners. A pop foul, two down. Lear has it all back, Lear thinks to himself. Anything now, just that last *out*.

McCannon checks the runners. So many, runners everywhere, if we ever get out of this—it's got to be a fast ball. His fingers dance, cleverly he signals, Lear nods, a soft light in his eye, Lear rocks back, McCannon looks up suddenly, to the sky—

The ball skids past him—"What!" he calls, running to the backstop, groping and fumbling as one run scores, another rounds third, looming, but McCannon has the ball, Lear covers the plate, the runner hesitates, the game is tied.

Lear burns, full of fury and fire, and the last batter is no challenge.

"If someone had come up to me, Ed, when I was starting out, and told me that all I would ever do in the Bigs was lose damn near every time out, second division every year, hell, back there playing with the Bucs, or coaching, managing, bush leagues and Bigs, just second division year after year—"

"You'd still be here."

"Sounds good, Ed. Pretty damn noble. Shit, what I coulda been. "

The ballgame plays on, Ralph makes the logical and unthinking moves, perfectly trained to the cliches of the game. He can see himself out on the field, self-assurance more than a match for reflex: 'You shoulda had that,' he can yell with perfect right. In mind's eye he himself played it flawlessly. On the field the real game goes into the ninth, all tied up.

Ralph watches the players trooping into the dugout. He points at Hardy, Macy and McCannon. "A run, men. One measly run. Do that. Hold 'em, and we're on our way. This ain't over, not by—" Ralph bounces on his toes.

Zeke Hardy wanders down the bench. He picks up a bat and leans against the dugout wall. He watches the field, the warm afternoon, infielders scampering after the ball, big slow pitcher warming up. Zeke stares, blank eyes, despair and acceptance, the players moving each time exactly as he knows they will once again, the pitcher floats the ball, Zeke watches, waiting—Ralph puts a hand on his shoulder.

"This is it, son." He points. "Just go with the pitch, pop the ball to right, get us a single. That's what we need. If you're feeling tired we can put Turle in to run, you know that."

Hardy nods. He knows.

"Now you're due up there. Show us proud, Zeke."

Hardy walks to the plate. He stops in the on-deck circle, squats and wipes his bat, watches the pitcher closely. The pitcher rocks back, whips the ball overhand and nods at the umpire. The catcher fires the ball back across the diamond and Zeke ambles up to bat.

Hardy stares at the stands far away. The game begins again. The stands, he sees, are painted green, a flat unnatural green, outfield grass lapping against the fences. In all his years Hardy has never played the outfield. He runs tight circles in the infield warming up. When the team takes their processional around the ballpark, he sits in the dugout with the coaches.

Hardy waits. The pitcher sets. Take the first pitch, they always say, take that first pitch because. They tell you that he will be wild, loose, unaccustomed, that he has to come to you, he's thinking and you're not. Take the first pitch. The infield will seize up, be tight on that second pitch when they have no release or action on the first pitch. Take the pitch. See what he has got, size him up, get the idea. Damn, twenty years in the game I've got a damn good idea.

He swings and misses, strike one.

Fans cheer. Zeke steps backward, readjusts his cap. The pitcher reads his catcher and moves. Hardy steps in and waits. Far away and dreamy, the pitcher releases his pitch, the ball floats and Hardy reads it perfectly, sees where the ball will break, and instantly, one split-second before it breaks, he swings—snap!—crack!, a cannonading line shot to left, solid base hit, Hardy runs down the line thinking base hit, maybe two with hustle, as he looks up—

The crowd gasps but is cut off like a knife. Kuenn the quick shortstop sprawls flat on his stomach with his gloved hand in the air, little bit of white against the tan like forbidden pudenda peeking out, the ball trapped, Kuenn looks beseechingly to the umpire and he in turn recovers, looks at Hardy laughing and gestures him out.

The inning ends with two more quick outs. Hardy picks up his glove, walks through the dusty infield to third base. He doesn't hurry. He's been around long enough and knows his limits. Hardy stops at third, pulls on his glove, pounds out a pocket in the leather. The ground around his base is cut with hundreds of triangle-claws, memories of runners and quick fielders, brief confrontations, decisions. Hardy kicks at the base, tied to a steel peg deep in the earth. He nods at Bunyan. "Sure you're ready now?," Bunyan calls, laughing, Hardy nods again and John tosses the infield ball, Hardy ambles in front of it, expert and graceless, smothers the ball in his glove and digs it out.

Zeke Hardy has been in baseball a long time.

Zeke Hardy played in the minor leagues for seventeen years before Ralph finally put him on the Senators' roster. Hardy had signed a bonus contract before he was out of high school and at first Ralph thought of him as too young. Then one spring Ralph saw him stumble chasing a ground ball and after that he was too old. Hardy kicks the dirt, tamps it down. One year Ralph took him north with the big-league team, expecting to make a coach or trainer of him. Hardy filled in for a few games at third early in the year when injuries thinned the squad, then made the lineup for good when he homered off Billy Pierce one hot day in Chicago. He hit two-fiftyfive that year, the same average he hits every year, bush leagues or Bigs.

Bunyan tosses the ball again, the game ball around the horn, another long looping throw, Hardy walks out to the mound and flips the ball to Lear. Zeke had been a senior citizen of a rookie, older than most of the regulars. He fits in solidly at third base, not flashy but always making the plays, Kaline leads off and taps the ball his way, Hardy scoops, sets and fires the ball across the infield.

One out.

Hardy has stories, stories he never tells, secret formless personal dreams past the reach of numbers, statistics, box scores. He sits in a bar in Prairie du Chien. He is playing his second year of pro ball, only eighteen, he looks his age but his age is always thirty. No one notices or speaks to him, day after day he comes in after the game, silent, day after day he reads the signs plastered behind the bar, ancient one-liners, 'In God we trust,' a saying, a phrase, dead words, 'all others pay cash,' and mother-in-law jokes, posters, nail-clipper displays, barn dance ads scattered across the green peeling walls, it all winds down, why, he wonders, why, only two years into the game and already he wonders, what is he waiting for.

Once a month he gets a baseball magazine. He brings it into the bar with him, sits on a stool and reads it cover to cover for two or three days. He pays special attention to the small ads in the back. Zeke can play ball for a long time but not forever, and when he retires he must have a new career, master another field.

Be a forest ranger. An expert in traffic control. Radio repair. Shorthand or hotel executives. Hypnotism. He can even finish high school by mail. Once a year he picks one out and sends away, studies the booklets they send him all season long, curled up in the back of a bus crawling across minor-league America, year after year, looking for a sign, a bit of personal meaning, what will come next in Zeke Hardy's life.

In the winter he works construction to stay in shape for the next season's baseball, works overtime to make up for the bush-league salary. He always drops the courses then, too tired at night to answer the nit-picking questions at the end of each chapter.

One day, he knows, he will find the right one. He imagines a small shop all his own after he retires, a small, square white-painted store, tiny but obviously prosperous, with a neatly lettered sign, "Zeke's," over the door. Now his age shows in tiny faults on the field and he knows he will have to find what he wants soon. This time he thinks he has it. Television repair. A brand-new field. And these people, he can tell, mean business. They don't put their product in a small column-inch ad buried in the back pages with the cartoons and story-endings, no. This is right up front and a full-color page, as big as the CPA and beer ads. A modern thing too.

The batter pops the ball high, the ball disappears into the blue sky for the briefest instant, drifts slowly down, Zeke measures the ball, doesn't hurry or think, patient, the ball drops into his glove, plop, he squeezes tight and pulls the ball out. Two down. He looks carefully at the ball then tosses it to second. He watches the clouds as the next batter digs in. The pitcher fires, the batter swings and the ball floats away, far away, deeper into the sky, into the stands, the ball game is over, three-two, Tigers.

"That was a close one, Ralph," long chorus reports after the game. They have filed their stories and now, like Ralph, have no place to go between games. They sit in the cold locker room, squat on desks and lean against the walls, dissect the game as they wait for the next, look for sweet reason on the physical field. "If you could win those close ones, you'd be right up there. Into the first division and maybe even contending."

"Right." Ralph smiles. What the long chorus never knows...

"If McCannon had held on to that pitch, the run wouldn't have scored and who knows? Without that—"

"Zuv hung that pitch to Masaryk, you know, over the season these things tend to even out." Ralph must answer in rote-cliche, no longer even a code. Long chorus will take him at face value. Ralph keeps his private dreams private, he can't tell them the first thing about mystery in the game, cause without effect, time and tide that "...hell you can't count on errors or nothing if you want to be in the game, it's the fundamentals, you have to get the basics down and everything else follows..." Small gives and takes, long chorus wants to know, to comprehend, the game but will never, never, Ralph has played the game, coached, managed and watched and sometimes he feels like an old disappointed priest and wants to say, "It's only a game."

"Hey, there's no way we shoulda lost that game. No way." Sut slumps in front of his locker. How can the game be so unfair? "We had it won, John."

"But we didn't. And no question about it either. Dropo hit that last ball so far they'll never find it. That's the game, Sut. Win some, lose twenty." John smiles. "You do have to wonder, though. It seems like we aren't meant to win."

"No, it's the breaks, the breaks like they say. But, hey, if Ralph had put *me* in the game…" Sut smiles. That game's done. There's a ball game soon, and after that another, all right.

Across the room Ramose puts batteries in his record player, a battered clumsy machine in blue plastic that plays a single 45, Ramose's only record, over and over. A trombone twists, pulls, wails darkly in the grooves while screaming bodiless voices chant, howl, pray "Garva home, home-a Garvee," drives the phrase over and over again, "Garva home," Ramose flips the record over and the trombones play but no voices. Ramose carries the record and the phonograph around the league with him, plays it incessantly, the record collects chips and scratches, dents in the tin speakers. Once in Chicago he dropped the whole assembly on a concrete floor but it still plays, again and again, strange music on a tear through a world of surface noise. The ballplayers are silent. Only Macy's die rolls and Ramose's music scratch the silence. The locker room is a tiny silent city, the lights yellow and hard.

Macy calls. "Hey, shut that thing down, Julie. We got us one hell of a series going here, can't be bothered. Sut! You ought to be over here watching. All you guy should—you'd learn something about the game." Macy sits at a card table, dressed in a towel, pointing at cardboard charts and booklets full of numbers, playing cards spread out before him.

Macy has a dice baseball game. He plays with the trainer or the equipment man, uses it to prove all his theories. He brings in envelopes of the game's finest teams, each reduced to pasteboard and numbers.

Sut walks across the room and sits in one of the chairs. Macy, dice in hand, pauses. "Could have gone either way this afternoon, Sut," he says. "You like to see a ballgame played like that." He tosses the dice, a big red one and a smaller white, heavily across the table, at a cardboard backstop. "Damn shame we had to lose—would you look at that!" Seth points to the cardboard game. "We played 'em tight out there, but them's the breaks. The way the game goes. We'll have to come back and show them Tigers in the second game."

"You're out of the inning, Seth. Your batter singled but he was out trying for the extra base." The trainer reads from the charts. He smiles and scratches his nose.

"What!" Macy pounds the table but in a moment he is smiling again, laughing. A cardboard game, he remembers. "We'll come back. I got me a team here that won't quit. Hey! Over here, Ed," he calls to Keyser. "You played against these guys. You know how it was." He waves two envelopes and hand them over. The envelopes are labeled '1906 Cubs' and '1927 Yankees.' "Those were the greatest ever, Ed. No teams better, ever. We're playing them off now."

Keyser played against these Yankees. In his memory maybe they are immortal, but back then he went out on the field and played. He remembers 1906 too, but not for any baseball. Time reaches back, turns secret corners: no numbers, statistics, not even photographs were this old in Ed's mind.

Macy talks 1906 baseball sure as if he'd been there. "Put these two on the field against each other and you know you're going to have a game!" Macy is a fan and a player, dice baseball and real.

"Every time, Ed, that good pitching will stop the hitting. And these Cubs had it, Ed." Macy knows the baseball laws but the trainer with the dice rolls snake-eyes, boxcars. In this game they shatter Macy.

Keyser reads from the charts. "Home run, double, home run, deep fly out to right. This is the famous Three-Finger Brown you talk about?"

"That will happen, Ed. On any given day. Hey, this game is in Wrigley, remember that. The wind's blowing out, that's the trick. See, this dice game has it all, Ed."

Bunyan walks over and looks at the line score. "Your club is losing, Seth. I thought you were supposed to be a pretty good paper manager."

"Hey, that's right, John, but I've got to tell you. These are the Yankees I'm playing against and they have Ruth. Babe Ruth, John. The Yankees is a sure thing, John. Back then, now and always."

John picks up Ruth's card. "It's only a piece of board, Seth." He flicks it. "Not even as thick as a bubblegum card. Couldn't even play a good hand of poker with it."

"John. That is Babe Ruth, the greatest player the game has ever known and a southern boy to boot. You don't go around confusing him with the jack of hearts. Now let's see that card, he's about due to bat."

Bunyan sets the card down, the trainer rolls the dice, three mighty swings and the card is out. "What!" says John. "Strike out!"

"Ship him out," Macy laughs. "When he can't do the job, ship him out. The American way. When he's no use to the team—"

"This is your great hero, Seth? The first slip-up and you want to can him?"

"Sentimentality isn't the first part of baseball, John," says Macy. "Not the first part or the last. Why, look what they did do to Ruth. He was the greatest player ever but when deals were brewing they didn't think twice. The Red Sox had him, he was a great *pitcher* then, he did it all. But they needed money so the New Yorkers bought him. And when he started costing them money, when he wasn't performing like they wanted, they just sold him down the river to the Boston nationals. He was going to be a show for them, he was losing his power but he was still Babe Ruth and they figured the National League cities wanted to see the man in action too."

"Hey, but the best thing I ever heard about in baseball," Bunyan interrupts, "about the Ruth, something Macy here said, was Ruth at bat once in the World Series and he calls his shot."

"'32," says Macy.

"Right, whatever year it was. There in the middle of a tight game, a close series, the whole damn country watching, Ruth at bat, he takes a strike, Macy says—neither of us were there, we didn't actually see the game—and Ruth holds up one finger, like 'Casey at the Bat.' Then he takes another strike and holds up two fingers. And then he steps out of the box to point at the right field bleachers. Damn if he doesn't slam the next pitch right where he pointed..."

"Longest ball ever hit in Wrigley..."

"Put himself on the spot and then took over the game, had it all under his control..."

"A screaming liner to a spot where no ball had been hit before..."

"Hit the most home runs, the longest home runs, the hardest-hit, slammed more in a season than entire teams, hundreds and hundreds lifetime..."

"Seven hundred and fourteen. There'll never be another Ruth."

Sometimes I did, said Ruth. Sometimes I didn't. Hell, it was fun. Time passes: Ruth becomes an easy out and later he dies.

"But later," says Macy, "at the end of his career when he was just about to pack it in, after they traded him over to Boston. See, he's batting just one-fifty, on his way down, out. The team's in last place and Ruth is doing nothing. He wants to quit but they tell him to stay for the last road trip, all the folks still want to see him. He wants to quit, sees no use, but he stays on. They go to Pittsburgh and damn if he don't hit *three* home runs in one game. Smash. Boom. He hits that last one, the last home run of his career, blasts the ball to right and over the double-deck stands, farther than anyone ever, see, six hundred feet and more.

"They wouldn't let him retire then, either. He had to play out the road trip, but after that home run he didn't get no hits or nothing. The last game he played, he hurt his knee chasing a fly ball in the first inning. He left and never played again.

"They say that last home run, he hit it so far that it's still going."

Ralph reaches across his desk for a loose ball. He turns it in his hand, tries different grips, fastball, slider, fork ball. All the things it can do, its twists and bounces, strange displacements on a diamond. The wonder of it is that any man can hit the ball squarely. Past that, a loose pebble, a flash of sunlight, catch a spike or a heartache, anything can happen, it's a wonder we can run the game at all. But we do.

Ralph picks up a pen and autographs the ball. He holds it at arm's length and turns it, examines his name scrawled against the strict seams. A hard surface, rough and real hide, a *fine* texture. It fits his hand so well—a solid thing, solid and real, definite meaning and definite limits. Nothing behind it, nothing inside it, only itself.

Yankees sign these, give away five and six dozen at a time. Sign balls for half an hour a day, that's part of their paycheck. Hell, we couldn't give away that many in a month. People are Yankees, people like winners.

Ralph autographs another ball. He sits back and looks at the schedule on the wall.

If they would give me the players...

Sometimes he walks through empty ballparks, alone in the early morning hours before batting practice, past surprising deep shadows among flat hard bolts of sunlight along the cement corridor, another time late at night after all the ballplayers have left, stops to lean against the cool concrete walls when he is tired. Stories run through him. He pauses before the last turn, before he is out of the stadium into the playing field in the bright sun or ghastly moon, watches the game from yesterday, the day before, sees every baseball day, batters, fielders, pitchers in a perfect dance...

"The stats, Ralph. Seems however we look at them, we lost the game."

Lock Graunt pushes a sheet of paper across the desk and smiles. Ralph sits up straight, shakes his head.

"But a game like that we can come back from," Lock continues. "A close game, a tight one, now that keeps the players on their toes. It's those one-sided affairs that chew up the bullpen, wear the players out for no cause, those are what we want to avoid."

Lock runs his fingers down the numbers. Ralph frowns.

"We picked up ten hits, turned some good plays in the field, we made ourselves a showing," says Lock. "Three-two, now that is something we can come back from. I'll bet the players are saying right now 'If only I'da…' "

"I'm sure they are, Lock. That's the kind of ballplayer we seem to have around here. If only. If only this, if only that. We got to shake them, Lock. They get a mouthful of maybe and that don't do us any good. We can't have them sit around talking, bitching, second-guessing everything. Play the game, let them figure out their mistakes, but none of this excuse shit. If only…

"We've got the horses, you see that, Lock. We've got—they have to get moving, that's all."

Lock doesn't answer.

"Once we get a few wins," says Ralph, "players will start to see what they're capable of."

They talk over the spare bones of the game. Every play reveals small insights to them, hidden resources on the club brought to light. What they are, what they need, what they might become. A good pitch in a tight spot will auger victories to come; the wrong pitch flattens the club for a week. Macy stumbles in the field one inning, flashes like sunlight the next.

"So Bunyan hit solidly every time at bat today, two long outs and three base hits. He's playing as well as he ever has and he's more consistent this season," Lock argues. "This season maybe, Bunyan could become one of the league's real stars."

Ralph nods seriously. Lock reads from the scorecard.

"And McCannon got a little single."

"Didn't lead to nothing."

"Hardy played solid, not an error, started a double play and stopped a few hard-hit ones."

"Popped up and lined out. We lost, Lock."

Lock shakes his head, full of worry and concern over the bounces of a ball. Lock knows baseball, knows the game's theory inside and out, the mechanics and the physics of the game. Ralph appreciates that. If ballplayers were machines, no one could tune them finer.

In his youth and beyond Lock had been a steady-fielding no-hit second baseman for twelve years in the minors and three days in the Bigs. Ralph played with him one year at Winston-Salem, then managed him ten years later at Savannah. He listened carefully as Lock expounded, talking for hours about play combinations, the Old Gag move, hints on intimidating, humiliating and bamboozling opponents and umpires, the mathematics of backup plays, the tiny details of the diamond come to life in exact forms as they rode in long buses, in late-night hotels, sat talking on the bench in forgotten games.

"We have to drill them, Ralph. That's how I see it. They made some of the simplest errors *again* today. Turle has no excuse for his baserunning. The batters have to learn again and again to hit *behind* the runner, advance him, keep out of the double play. Some bad choices on the pitch selection. McCannon's been around some but it looks like he just plain **forgot** a couple things. Teach them again, work on 'em, that's the ticket."

"Right, Lock. Get them looking sharp." Ralph picks up the stat sheet and looks at it intently. He waits for Lock to leave.

"Say, Ralph, did you see that TV show last night?" Lock waits in the doorway. He smiles, not fondly, remembering.

"Gleason? Sure, I watched that. Keyser and McCannon come up to the lounge and we took it in. They had Gleason and Norton, those crazy fools, looking for this diamond ring they lost, see—"

"No, not that one." Lock waves his hand quickly. "This was later on, they had that senator on the television again. You know, McCarthy. Hey, that was a show!"

"Yeah. That one. No, I missed it, Lock. It was on too late and I went to bed."

"Well, you missed quite a show. You know, the old boy didn't miss a trick." Lock folds his arms across his stomach and leans against the door frame. "Some of the ball club is mighty big on him. You hear them talking all the time. Macy, Hardy, McConnell, a lot of them. The Catfish is a big fan too. Did you know the Commies got ahold of his father once? Over there in Hungary, Yuso-glavia, somewhere. He had to sneak out later in a car trunk. I guess he didn't like to talk about it too much and I can't say I blame him. You know about those Reds, don't you, Ralph?"

"Sure. Sure I do, Lock. I also know if we keep our asses in a sling we can move up to sixth place before we leave town so let's stay in the game, all game long. OK?" Ralph's Joe McCarthy is the game's Joe McCarthy, solid citizen Yankee manager.

Lock backs out of the office, looks around the club house then steps quickly back in. "What—say, what time do you figure we'll be taking infield tonight?"

Ralph smiles, drums his fingers on the table. "Usually for a night game we'll be out there about six-thirty or so. Just a short one tonight, though. We've played a game already. And let's look sharp out there, ok? Get some pride going and we can come back and beat hell out of those Tigers. What do you say, Lock?"

The stadium lights wink on bleakly. Dramatic corners of daytime shadow slowly dissolve and the diamond begins to float above the field. Now hard light shines everywhere and nothing in the ballpark is hidden. The late blazing sun and the evening sky fade away behind huge arc lamps, crackling and fussing: pure electricity spurts into the air. Blue ghosts dance the basepaths as the ground crew readies the field.

Inside the concrete locker room Macy's thin voice drones, Bunyan laughs, Ramose plays his music, the ballplayers wait.

Cott jumps up suddenly. An idea, a word in the air has struck him. "If they was to come asking me, I'd tell them all I know. That's your right, your patriotic duty." He nods vigorously, old and serious in his youth. "Anything they want to know, hey, tell them everything you've heard. These are the people that run the country, you know. Tell them everything. Even the rumors, that's how facts start out. Give them something to follow up on. Something, hey now, maybe you don't think it means much, but these guys are the pros, they know how to follow up on that shit."

Andy Cott, the kid catcher, pushing shoving kid, always running but not fast enough, hustles to back up the play at first base but too late, runs out to warm up the pitchers, shags for the coaches, pitches batting practice to the bench. "Hey boss," he calls. Of four hundred major leaguers, he ranks in the high three-nineties. He tries, shoves, fat and obtrusive. The game's rewards, he says, are life's rewards, and just as much out of reach. Push! Reach! You're in the game! 'Hey boss,' he says, and happy to say it, up in the Big Show.

"That's how I see it, boss, we got to pull together."

"I favor Cobb," Ralph says.

"No, Ralph, I'm afraid you're off target there. Cobb was great but he couldn't change, he got outmoded, let the game pass him by. He never did adapt to the power game. You have to stay with the game," Lock explains. "He was the leader of those great Tiger teams, pennant winners for a time, true enough. But he played twenty years past that without a winner. And twenty years is a long time."

The coaches, Lock and Ed, stand in Ralph's tiny office, rub back against the rough green cinderblock while Ralph sits in his chair, feet-up. McCannon, freshly showered after the game, leans on the door frame.

"The thing was," Lock continues, "after they invented the lively ball and the way Ruth played, there was no call for—"

"Horseshit," says Ralph. "Cobb was never outmoded. The teams he was on couldn't play the game, couldn't keep up with the man, there's your problem. Cobb didn't have the material to work with. The players didn't know the inside game. He had to have a good smart team to play his style, heads-up players like Wahoo Sam Crawford and Donnie Bush, like the men he had with him in the early days. When he's surrounded by ordinary players, of course the team's not going to do much. Hell, with Ruth and that power you could put eight nuns on the team and still win games. But it's sloppy, Lock, it's not true. That game isn't the *real* baseball game.

"I've seen Cobb play, I've played against him. He took the game, just took it over. Every base was *his*, every game was *his* game. All his, you didn't figure in it at all. He had every man afraid of him.

"There's two ways you can go about the game, Lock. Power or finesse. With power you want to just blow the other team away, hope they won't do the same to you. But the close game, the inside game, you've got all the elements working together and you get more than the sum, you get the entirety of the game.

"When it's Cobb you've got on base, or Max Carey, George Case, any of the really good runners like the Minoso now, they'll knock a single, get on first—a home run, swish bang, it's all over. Now Cobb gets on base, he'll take his lead, dare the pitcher, jump, make little moves in the corner of the pitcher's eye and the man on the mound starts thinking, the fielders are pulled out of their normal positions and trying to guess with the runner, is he going or not, the backup plays, who covers, where the hole will be. And the catcher, the man who should be keeping the team together out there, he thinks just fast ball, he wants to get the throw off quick to nail the runner. When you've got a team out there *thinking*, guessing against you and not just playing, Lock, that's when you've got them on the run."

"Right," says Keyser.

"Now, the home run team," Ralph continues, "they need every man be a threat. If only one or two have the power, you can pitch around them. But a team full of runners—"

"Just a track meet," says Lock. "Now if you don't think the sight of that little ball as it disappears into the stands doesn't do something to the pitcher—"

"At least he isn't thinking." Ralph laughs, wipes his mouth. "He made a mistake and now he can start over fresh."

"No, I like to see power action in a game, Ralph. A good show. The ball blasted far, far away and men trotting around the bases, coming in to score. Good, solid, hitting."

"Nah, the game's a balance, Lock," says Ralph. "See it my way. You got to have it all. You're not going to win if your power hitter lets in more runs with his glove than he drives in with his bat. Pitching, that's the greater part of the game anyway. Build the offense around that. We don't have no pitching and see where we sit. And there's defense."

"You've got to have it all, the corners and the inside game. When everyone on the field is *with* the game, playing for all it's worth, that's when you really see the game, what the game can be.

"Cobb knew how to get into the game, he took the game, controlled the action, the flow, kept running and everyone's eyes were on him all game long. A man like that, Lock. You don't outmode Cobb.

"Gentlemen, I see game time is upon us." Ralph smiles. Today's game, not yesterday's. "Leave us take our fine crew of baserunning demons and power fiends out to the diamond and shake things up. Get *into* the game!"

"McCaslin!" Ralph shouts. "Do us proud! You're out in right tonight!" Ralph herds the ballclub out of the locker room toward the diamond. Something is up. Sut smiles, uncertainly. They walk down the long ramp and Bunyan points across the field.

"They're throwing us to the lion, Sut. Old Jack Slade is pitching."

Old Jack Slade, 'the oldest story in baseball,' will be on the mound for Detroit tonight. Slade has been around the game for a long time, pitching in the majors since the early 'Thirties. Today he pitches to Mantle and Minoso while through him baseball connects directly to DiMaggio, Greenberg, Gehrig, Slade's contemporaries, to Ruth and Johnson and they carry the game back in earlier generations to Cobb and Speaker, Wagner, Cy Young to King Kelly and past them to baseball's very first, forgotten and nameless. Slade is direct descent, the pure energy of the game, movement on the empty basepaths, pulses in the air.

The Tigers are on the field, the reserves stand waiting in the dugout. The stands buzz with pregame excitement. Gardiner the manager hurries out with a mitt while the catcher fumbles with his buckles.

Slade is a small man warming up but the ball comes in like a bullet fired by a giant. Slade leans forward, he stretches, rocks back, he whips the ball, inspires a crackling white life dead across the plate. The ball pops out of the mitt and rolls away. Slade watches. His forehead juts, solid as a rock. His chin pushes at an angle. He always looks at the plate sideways. Slade doesn't lose often.

His past—where did Slade come from? Who is he? Human interest, long chorus asks. Does he visit dying kids in hospitals, did he ever chase fire engines? The young man growing up, destined for greatness; what was he like? They know Slade only as the full-grown man come out of nowhere to create a timeless 27-3, 1.06 ERA season at Galveston in the Texas League in 1929, sold to Cleveland for a king's ransom and pitching year after year, suddenly one of baseball's constants. They hold him in the record book and the sports pages but no stories outside baseball for long chorus.

Twenty-three years in the Bigs, says long chorus (in the game they know him well), almost thirty in the pros, his mere longevity an enviable record but more than that, much more. This season he stands on the verge of breaking one of baseball's oldest, grandest records, the finest a pitcher could hope for: Slade is only sixteen wins short of Cy Young's all-time record, five hundred and eleven wins in one mortal career.

This season, says Slade. This year.

Not long ago long chorus had given up on Slade. He had the wins, over three, over four hundred but then he lost a few games, was traded away from Cleveland, lost again, traded again. The Tigers, a hungry team, dealt youth for Slade and brought him to Detroit. That first year he lost five more games, rapidly. The players were new, young, faceless. Slade pitched without nuance, without knowledge, purely experimenting.

Slade crosses the foul lines and waits for the game to begin. No doubt now, says long chorus. It's over. Slade pauses to listen while long chorus drives the final nails (but Slade knows): He's getting old. When he is young he can do anything but now…

Slade picks at the baseball. He looks at the men, fat men in baggy suits speaking about him but never to him, a shouted question, 'How does it feel…' and the men edge further away, looking about them for some-thing new, a new story. Slade straddles the mound. He understands.

Four hundred and forty-two lifetime wins but oh-and-five this year. This is it, Jack, they had told him. Seventy wins are a lot to make up. A hell of a lot, thinks Slade. He will never make it, long chorus decides. Ten and twenty-four, eight and sixteen with the poor Cardinals and now nothing and five with Detroit.

Look, they say, grabbing you lightly by the collar and looking into your eyes, he'd have to win twenty a year or better and even then it will be years, hey, he's old and not game one has he won this year. He'll be pitching from a wheelchair soon. The legs.

Slade takes his glove off, rubs the ball in his bare hand. Roughly, he pushes at it with his palms. He spits on the ball and rubs that in too. Slade is newly strong, now wonderful and terrible, reborn on the mound. He has but one view, life's razor edge so sharp in his mind: Five hundred and twelve lifetime wins. The game can't deny him, Slade has no more feelings but there is a force inside him, the game, the old ideas and patterns, the next game ahead. Slade senses the old strengths returning, rushing through his veins, pounding, insistent.

But long chorus has a deadline. Slade's getting old, they say, well hell, he's been old for years. Had his thirtieth birthday four years running. Must be forty-well...It's that simple. The fattest one rubs at his chins. You can see it in the way he runs, the time he takes between pitches. Never see him do his wind sprints. And he can't slip the fast ball past Father Time, they say. They take cold numbers and find new meanings, certainties. Amazing while it lasted, they say to one another. Will we ever see another like him? We'll never see another Cy Young, that's for sure.

Baseball is a world of memory and a world of performance, says long chorus. One or the other, Jack, they tell him. Your past has been good, you've had the great years, the glory was yours and you'll be in Cooperstown, no sweat. But those days are gone. Hang it up, Jack.

He's still got the arm, the speed, he brings that back every year, says long chorus. The curve, the chageup. Those are real. And he's got more upstairs than anyone in the game. He won't lose that, they say. He can hang in there for a few more wins, pitch short relief, some patsy starts, the Browns and Washington maybe. Finesse 'em (They go to the games and they see Slade pitch, real and physical on the mound, but they only understand him in a boxscore, tiny view). There's a few wins, they say, another season or so, but seventy wins! There are human limits. Only so far you can go in the game. They let go your collar, back away and take a sip of their drink then with an understanding wink they say again, The legs. The legs are the first to go.

Slade looks at them. He knows what they are trying to say—when you're young there is nothing to stop you, just drive straight ahead and hit them with all you've got, youth without guile—but Slade's been around for a long while and youth is the last thing he knows. He studies the limits and the size of the diamond, lives the game like an ancient worshiping priest in stone hallways.

But no dogma for Slade. He works, fusses, shapes the baseball world around him. Before a game he sharpens his belt buckle, then quickly gouges the ball during the game, strange symmetry makes the ball flutter and dip, the batter pops up or strikes out sprawling. When the umpire admonishes Slade and throws the ball out, the catcher runs the ball over his shin guards, bright shiny sharp parts, and Slade is dueling again. He has a thousand answers for every question, he cán see the one win five hundred and twelve times.

Slade looks at long chorus one last time, distant in the press box, then tugs at his glove and turns to the batter. The White Sox, Red Sox, A's and Indians, the American League—Slade runs off twelve straight victories, recovers baseball's strength, a streak and a wheel rolling of itself through the league until Reynolds stops him 1-0 in New York. Then Slade is off again to a dozen more wins, twenty-four on the season and a new career, an old man's scattered bones brought back to life. Long chorus takes a step back. What is this?

The second year with Detroit he won thirty.

No one! they scream in bars, the noise pulsing and crashing in waves when Slade is on the television, he glaring and spitting, beating the White Sox and the Senators five times each! No one, not since Lefty Grove back when we all were kids, and this is history being made, more than history, sixteen more wins this coming season and Cy Young is forgotten, Jack Slade the new measure of the game.

Slade masters the league, knifelike and slim on the mound. He breaks every record, the baseball in him transforms baseball. His picture, Slade scowling, vicious and picking at his fingernails, is on every magazine cover. Slade cruises toward the new record, no one can stop him but he plays on a team, a mortal aggregation and he can't pitch every game, the team struggles, the Tigers finish that season in third place. The Yankees spreadeagle them by thirteen games. No World Series this year, not in Detroit.

Long chorus stands around silently, tired and confused, so excited but it passes, now a cold winter, memories of what might have been. They switch the TV over to another picture, huge men wrestling,

Randolph Scott riding across the tiny blue screen, roller derby and there's Toughie and Jean Porter going at each other again, and that senator's show, they say. Now there's a man who's got something, don't you think?...

Five hundred and twelve, one goddamn more than Young, Slade thinks. This far into the new season and given up for dead two years back. Now it's a sure thing. No one else even close, the pitcher will *never* be born to beat this record.

Slade taps his chest, bounces on his heels on the pitcher's rubber. Tom Bartlett twirls his bat, bends to touch his toes and stands in at the plate. The first Senator batter.

On the mound Slade does not look like a figure of history. Tobacco swells one cheek. He rubs his unshaven black stubble and spits solidly, once, toward third base and then faces the batter. When the duel starts he does not spit again, holds or might even swallow the tobacco, all his attention centers on the strike zone, the fluxing ideal in space, the delicate ebb and flow as the batter stretches, cuts the air, settles and waits. Then Slade and baseball go to work.

No one crowds him either. In his career he has hit two hundred and forty-six batters, another all-time record.

Slade moves easily through the Senators' lineup, dances pitches past the first ten batters before Petrarkis taps the ball just past the second baseman's glove into short center. Slade takes the ball and flips it high in the air, catches it without looking as he stares at Petrarkis. Hardy hits the ball into the soft dirt and Petrarkis the Speedy is in at second.

Bunyan walks to the plate. He's known Slade a long time. He ducks back on the first pitch, stares in sudden wonder at the next then drives a shot to right, Slade was slow or cute, Petrakis moves, The Speedy spurts around third, dives down the basepath and slides headfirst and under the rough tag, rolls over and bounces up laughing, runs back to the plate and taps it again.

Sut is due up. He swings his bat and looks at Slade. Back in the second inning Slade had pitched to Sut and the ball floated gently, Sut swung and hit it well, high, but neither well nor high enough and Kaline caught the ball on a slow lope.

Sut kicks at the dirt around the plate. Slade will throw the first one at me since we scored on him. Got to keep my right foot back so I can get out of the way quick.

Slade stands on the mound, Sut stares, Slade far away holds the ball cupped in his hand and waits. Sut waits. Slade stares at his catcher, stares at the plate, the zone, Sut moves but Slade doesn't see, Slade looms in the hot evening, shimmers in the heat, Sut stares and waits, Slade shimmers in the heat, the slow hot wind through the ballpark, Sut waits, Slade ripples and moves, heat waves and light, motion on the mound as if he were no real Slade at all...

The ball sings. Sut backs quickly away. The pitch cuts the plate. Lock Graunt pulls at his cap. Ralph screams in the dugout. "Back in the game, McCaslin. Getcher head back in the game!" Bunyan on base laughs. Sut swings his bat and steps in again, crowds the plate a little. We'll come back. What the hell, it's only a game.

Slade stares.

Maybe it's this one, and the ball drives at him, solid and angry, Sut ducks away as the ball in cruel english slices back across the plate.

Damn. Sometimes you feel like a little kid in this game.

The next pitch burns with no pretense, no artifice, nothing but real speed, the umpire growls That's three yer outta there.

"He just gets better and better the longer he pitches, Sut." Bunyan leans back in the ramp outside the dugout. Out of Ralph's sight they sneak a cigaret. "I don't know how he's kept it in him. I remember batting against him once when I first come up, before the war. And he'd been around a long time even then."

John takes a long drag off the cigaret and tosses it against the far wall. It hits the sharp plaster and sticks, a small and useless miracle. "See that, Sut? Dead solid perfect. You don't see that every day. Put it in the record books.

"Now Slade says he's gonna retire after that last win. Just to get one above Cy Young and quit."

"He says that but I don't know. Suppose the Tigers were up there in the race come September? He wouldn't quit then."

"I don't think he'll have any pennant to worry over. Not after last year, when he pulls down thirty wins and they still finish way back in third. But even if they were in the race, I think old Slade would still hang it up."

"If I had his stuff, hey, I'd sure keep it up as long as I could. You wouldn't see me retire until they cut my uniform off." Sut smiles. Once, long ago, he saw himself doing just that, playing in the leagues forever, across all the generations of ballplayers, become a story and a standard.

"Right. You'd be the all-time plowjockey." Bunyan laughs. "No, Slade's been around a long time. He's there, he'll make his record easy this year. He's got *this* game in his pocket."

"We're ahead, John. Christ!" The game, thinks Sut.

"Only by a run. He was weak last inning. If that's all the better we can do when he doesn't have it together, well…He just gets stronger over a game, like he gets stronger over a season and damn near unbeatable over the career. A good thing he *is* quitting."

"Hey, no game is over until the last out." Sut believes this. He has to say it nakedly, a small important article of faith. "We're ahead, if we can stay ahead, simple as that, we've got him beat. Didn't Ralph teach you that?"

"Right, Sut."

Slade retires the last batter of the inning and the Senators take the field, Sut grabs his glove and runs far into the outfield, runs hustling miles away from the dugout and the score and the rules, throws a ball to Tom Bartlett in center, takes the return throw and then heaves with all his strength, fires a strike across the outfield to the right fielder, smiles and laughs and flexes his arm, new strength, and on the diamond the game begins again—

Batter at the plate. Sut squints, runs through the Tiger lineup in his mind. Walt Dropo. When he's up, we shade him 'way over to left. So I'm almost on the line. He's a dead pull hitter. Or is that the other way? Where's Bartlett playing? He's way over this way too, but he might be covering for me. If I play straight-away, maybe Tom will move over too. Or wave me back. Dropo's got to be a pull hitter. He's been in the league a few years now and they like that kind. Don't know why. What's the count? Dropo looked awful foolish on that last pitch. Shouldn't Macy relay the count? Or he only signals the outs. But Kaline—no, Dropo's up, he's taking. The Tigers have to catch up. Keep the ball inside, make him go to right. Do me a favor.

Dropo swings, a jerky compacted stroke, the ball lofts slowly into the air, a stately fascinating object, Sut watches but Bartlett runs and yells "Sut, Sut," oh it's all mine. Sut turns, runs, blind and instinctive, one moment he feels every pound, every cigaret but suddenly he bursts free and runs like a kid again, sticks his glove high and a little jump and snap!, his wrist jerks, he opens his eyes and there is the ball, stuck to his glove. Sut turns casually and tosses the ball to Bartlett. We're professionals, yes we do this all the time. And even a blind gopher can find the acorn.

"Nice catch," says Bartlett.

Slade pitches relentlessly, the Senators cannot hold and the Tigers tie the game, edge ahead, score more runs and burst ahead, five, seven, eight to one. Another win for Detroit—how many in a row! The shortstop pounds his glove and wishes, a good series here and off and running, the outfielders smile and think this might be their year. The bench cheers. Slade, alone on the mound, pitches.

Sut digs his spikes into the soft dirt, leans back in the batter's box and taps the far corner of the plate with his bat. Buckle down. Don't want to go fishing now, the game's not over yet, a base hit could score a run and we'd be on our way back. A rally against Jack Slade, all right. He's seen it all. Get this game turned around. Sut smiles. He looks across the diamond at the pitcher, takes a short practice cut, pulls the bat back and tenses.

Just a pop, just a base hit, little bingo, done it before and we can do it again. Goddam, how about it. Meet the ball, go with the pitch, take it to right…Off Slade.

Slade stares down the plate.

Sut waits. He tenses, squeezes the bat, relaxes, watches Slade. Sut wants to scratch the back of his leg. Just step out. What's Slade going to throw? Slade moves, slowly, stops at the top of his motion and stares at the baserunner, moves…Sut can't move. He waits. Slade is careful and smooth, rare, ancient, he moves smoothly and brings the ball in effortless overhand…

The pitch was outside but Sut doesn't know. The catcher tosses the ball back before Sut realizes what has happened. He digs in again, kicks the dirt, reaches his bat out and taps the plate. Settles. Swings the bat. Waits.

Twice more the pitch is outside. Slade stands on the mound with the ball, right hand tightly clasped, arms hanging at his side. He spits, dismal brown juice.

I'm a gonna lose the bastard.

Sut is taking all the way. A walk's as good as a hit, he remembers. They told him that even in high school. Sandlot knowledge.

Slade stares. He checks the runner. He reaches back so far and brings the ball fast and smooth and cruel—

Sut knows it's coming. The ball is on the way, somewhere, but Sut doesn't see it until thwack! with a dull thud the ball explodes off his back like heavy thunder, throws him sprawling across the plate—

Hardy sits on a stool and watches. The television picture rolls slowly, then stabilizes. We could have fixed it. Nothing easier once you know how. Lesson twelve. Finished that one three weeks ago.

Another game. Some day there won't be another but I'll be ready for that.

McCarthy points to him, direct and personal. Right you are, sir, says Hardy. Without televison you might never know. You turn a TV set around and the only thing you see is a big stenciled sign. Do Not Remove Cover. Wired to Prevent Tamper. You don't just jump into a thing like that. You have got to know your way around. Be trained. Professional. Your average layman couldn't do it, would most likely only kill himself. Ha. Get one hell of a shock anyway.

Zeke looks at his hands. Thirty years playing ball, they've been trained, have a life of their own. A professional's hands. A surgeon's, a pianist. Crushed and gnarled. And now, the future ahead, all your life you work for one thing but it passes.

They explain to you how to get inside the set. How to open it up, the right way. What to watch for and what not to touch. Some of those tubes can stay hot for hours, the wrong move and they'd blow you right out of there. Study the set. Trial and error, but know what you're doing every step of the way. Watch yourself close. Once you become trained— so few make it this far, to Lesson Twenty.

All those tubes. Hardy ponders, slides his beer from one hand to the other on the bar. You've got to know which ones to look after, it's a regular forest in there. All those wires strung from here to there, tubes of all shapes, they're transparent so's you can see the insides although you'd never understand, it's all so complicated and the workings of a tube, an individual tube, no, something I'll get to later, something you don't have to know just yet. Take it on faith, so's you'll know which to replace and which not to touch. That much will stand you a good start in the business. Experience, you'll learn, they'll come to you with their TV sets and you will learn. Later, you'll know it well.

Pull off that cover for the first time. Looks pure chaos but there is true order before you, the wires connect and give one another meaning, there are the tubes, cause and effect, a wondrous pairing, a marriage of objects that holds, everything that can happen does happen. There is flow through all entrances, sensual movement, beams pulsing, electric organisms shot through a strait gate, a narrow way and there are charges, counter-forces, just like in the game, smaller and larger. Ralph speaks, Zeke follows, in his mind's eye there exists a heavenly field of iridescent electricity, vibrant colors and positive ion beams of God's pure love, a shimmering palpitating vision past physical shapes, pure joy awaiting him…

Zeke himself has been on the TV picture. A neighbor took a flash photo of the screen and although nothing was recognizable Zeke kept the picture, put it away in a box of other photographs.

"Hardy!" Macy yells. "Who was it that the Yanks picked up from us in that trade along with Noren? Been trying to think of his name all afternoon. Remembered he was down there at Savannah with you." The baseball world is small and Zeke must make a living. He shrugs.

"Been a few years."

"Hell." Macy pulls on a sports jacket, dark blue with gangster's lapels. "Not important. Keyser would know. Hey, let's get out. The TV show's over, McCarthy done give us the word. Let's find Bunyan and them and get some kicks in tonight."

"No, no, can't. Too much celebrating this week as it is. Have to find time to study tonight." Priorities, responsibility, they take on deadly order in Zeke's mind tonight. He watches Macy step out the door.

"And that Kincade. The Pride of Pittsburgh. I tell you." Macy takes another drink, his eyes bug, he points, bright neon paints him yellow, vivid orange, pulsing red. They stand surrounded by machines and the roar of heavy metal. "Christ, Kincade, he could have been one of your greats. The man had it. He had the wrists, such control. He had it all, boys. He could stop that ball dead, just lay it out, right there on the flipper. Dead as a mackerel. *Whenever* he wanted to. That Kincade, see, the man had it."

"Whatever happened to him, Seth? Did he drop off the circuit or what?" Bunyan looks at the half-naked women, demented gnomes, conquering heroes and the numbers, huge numbers, towering totals, numbers roll round and round, into the tens of thousands, violent lurid cartoons looming over every machine, blasts of wicked light. A man at the far end of the narrow room sells beer in paper cups while serious men in groups and pimply kids stand around the pinball machines. "Whatever did happen to Kincade, Seth?"

"Kincade. They all know Kincade. No one could handle 'Three Ducks' like that man. Once, hey, one night I saw him turn it over twice. Twice…in the same game. You just can't do that. Impossible, they say. A man can scarce beat it, let alone turn the machine over. But I saw Kincade do it." Macy shakes his head. "I don't know what happened to him." He looks at them. "I just don't know."

Sut points down the hallway. "Let's grab some more beers and get started. See what games are open. Maybe they have 'Pastime.' That's a good one."

"Why don't you go ahead and pick one out, Seth," Bunyan says. "I'm sure you know them all."

Seth nods sharply and hurries down the room and points at each machine. "This one—'Snakepit.' Lots of color, high scores, but not all that much action. No drop targets, hardly any bumpers. A simple game, real primitive. No.

"Now here's a civil war type of game. 'Brother against Brother.' See, here you can trigger extra balls so's you can get two, three rolling at once. Buttons to hit, a spinning dial, the works. Quite the machine. But look at the free game total! Hey, you want to be able to beat the machines, not just play on 'em. No, not this one.

"Here's 'Lost in the Flood.' Played this once in a back room in New York. Private place, the law frowns on these machines up there. But you've got to float the ball way up here," he points to a gutter high on the right, "and just hope that it drops in, if you really want to score. Takes too much faith.

"But here!" Seth jerks, darts, hurries over to a huge gaudy machine in a row of huge gaudy machines. "This is my favorite." Bunyan drops nickels down a chute. Macy presses a button and takes the first game.

'Ahab the White Whale,' the machine is named and there sure enough is the great whale, bulbous and round, floating on the horizon line with a broad inane smile, a spout over his head like an umbrella. In the foreground stands part of a whaling ship, mast and foredeck in wild perspective. Up the mast a man with a small telescope waves and points while on the deck a tall sepulchral figure with a yellow wooden leg stares at the fish.

Sut watches Macy play the first game. He usually waits until last himself so he can get an idea of the game. "The damn flippers are slow," Seth growls. "Got to be careful with this one. Now watch what I do."

Near the top of the board a small white-whale fish light flashes from one bumper to another, a lighted panel that seems to move randomly. If the bumper is hit when the whale's light sits there, the ball pulls a considerable bonus. Sut watches the game, the ball, bright colored lights spun out into the night, fantasy in a crowded smoky hallway where all the machines teach a single weary lesson. The whale moves erratically, lingers on one bumper then flies over the board at impossible speeds, pauses and alternates back and forth on the top two bumpers.

If I can figure the pattern, see what button does this, what does that, that's how you rack up the points. Sut sets his beer on a small table. If I study it, watch John and Macy go at it, maybe I can figure how it goes. There's a pattern there, got to be a pattern.

"Did I tell you about the time Weber challenged Kincade to a shoot-out? That was back in Kincade's one great season, that championship season, that year he just swept through all the bars and arcades, when he even challenged Weber's great single-season percentage. Kincade was clipping along at a sold 120%, 125%—they figure it on your score for each league game, compared to the free game total for that particular machine, see.

"Now he's at one-twenty-whatever with the season half done, and this is when the league average is 67%, 68%. And Weber's great season mark is 98%. That's damn close, but no man has ever been able to *average* a free game, see, every time out over a whole season. And Kincade has the chance, he's playing so far above the mark, it was just amazing.

"He'd walk into a bar, right away you would just *know*. Nothing phony about this man, see. He's walk right up to the pinball. If there was anybody playing, they would stop, back away from the machine, let the man have it. Don't mess with the Killer.

"Weber was the old champion, see, he'd won the Grand Nationals three years running, Weber was the king but he looked like he was slipping. Kincade was on the way. This Kincade is almost a rookie, just a kid out of nowhere. Weber saw it coming and then he challenged."

Macy loses a ball. He looks up from the table in profound disgust. "Right smack between the flippers. Nothing you can do, the ball's just lost, all your skill to vain.

"So Weber wanted a shoot-out, see. And it was to be on this very game, too. In the Baltimore Play Barn. Weber wanted to have it on the line, all spelled out. Who was the champ, see. Show this kid who the man was."

So this is a shoot-out. Macy's stories were much better when Sut hadn't realized they were about pinball.

"Straight high total, see. You add up the scores from all the games you play. And you include in all the free games you get for matched digits too. Now in league games these don't count, because you get them random. So you just play them out for practice. The only ones that count there are the ones you pay for or *earn*.

"But in a shoot-out everything goes. Gives the deal a little chance, see. And you can win free games off a those free games, more and more, watch the score pile up. Now you get these games pure random, see, and Weber, he's been the king all along so he figures they'll be his. The luck will be with him, he'll carry all the match wins." Macy slaps the side of the machine, twists and jerks, applies elaborate and useless english. The ball slips away down the gutters and scoring ends.

"They were both real experts on this game. And it's a good one for a challenge, too. See, the game's too tough for league play and you have to be damn good to play it right. Plus which it's fun. You have to be both good *and* lucky. Ahab up there, see, was the whale that swallowed Jonah. A classic game." Macy pulls the plunger and sets a new ball into play. "See? Now just keep it moving. You never know where the big scores are on this game."

"A challenge born of chaos," says Bunyan.

"What? No, just keep it rolling. You're bound to hit something. See!" Deep chimes toll, Macy's score, posted in the belly of the whale, rolls round and round, impossibly high numbers, the ball dances happily across the board. "But that wasn't Ahab that I hit. When that happens, hey, you *know* you've scored!" Seth dances with the ball. "Yeah, Kincade coulda been one of the great ones. I saw him on this game once, maybe he got Ahab, maybe he didn't, I don't remember—"

"How did the shoot-out go, Seth?"

"The shoot-out?" Macy stares at the board and follows his tiny reflection in the rolling ball. "Hey, that was the damnedest thing. Kincade never showed up and we didn't see hide ner hair for two years. Turns out he was a pro bowler too and got called away to a big tourney up in Milwaukee somewhere. Got hot and played all up and down the Midwest for years.

"But look at that! Would you look at that damn ball!"

Sut watches. Macy, wired to the machine, crawls under the glass and rolls 'cross the board with the ball. He crashes into lights, nine hundred, one thousand, bounces off pillars, twelve hundred, careens into posts, bang bang bang. Fifteen hundred and forty, fifty, more. He's sure to find Ahab.

"See! Just got to score a thousand on the next ball!" Macy turns round grinning, a thin fine line of sweat across his forehead, a light in his eye. "Got the machine down for the count! We're going in!"

The games are over. Metal buzzes, clappers snap, circuits jam and the score rolls 'round in hundreds, in thousands, but the players come up short, the free games run out and they are down to beer money. "We're ballplayers—you know," Macy announces to the crowd and the self-educated man joins them. He wants to buy drinks for them.

"Baseball—yes?" The self-educated man points to a booth in the small tight bar. They push past jammed-up tables, spaces open and close before them, a woman laughs sharply and turns away, toward the middle of the night they reach the booth. The self-educated man waves at the bartender, waves green dollar bills.

"Hey, I guess you know this much," Macy says. He wants to tell the man everything he knows. "This is the game, hey, it's the game we've been in for so many years, one of the nation's true glories, been the same game almost forever. It's like truth, hey. Something you'd *know*. Men have played this game, known all the true facts and strategies, since Day One. Once they laid those basepaths out, see, that was the secret. Then they had it all.

"The way it came about, see, one day—back in the old days they were playing games, sure, but just *games*, nothing real. One of the men—and later this same guy was a Yankee general in the Invasion, and then after that he was on the first train west to California—well, he set the game out, the *entire* thing, all at one time.

"He saw the game there in his mind, like a dream or a vision or something, and put down the right distances, your ninety-foot basepaths exact. That was one of the secrets, see. So that the game was perfectly balanced, you could win on offense, see, or you could win on defense because, see," Macy pauses, sips his drink, straightens in his chair and looks the man cold in the eye. "The time it takes the batter to run to first is almost exact the same time that the fielder needs."

Men pass in a crowd, press against their booth, hot night, rough wool and bursts of cigaret smoke, hoarse laughter and coughs, the group moves on and the bar opens up, suddenly a wider world. Macy sits smiling and satisfied, the noble bearer of Truth.

"I don't know, Seth," says Bunyan. "Seems to me you're pretty consistently behind the runner. Maybe I should kick the bag a few feet back when the ball goes your way."

"No, no, that's the whole idea!" Macy stands partway and poses. The self-educated man watches closely, excited, looks from one player to another. He winks broadly at Sut. "We don't win because the team don't shape up to standards," Macy says. "It's that simple, see. They call it fundamentals. The people that can play the game, really *play* the game, they're the ones who are up there. Gil McDougald, Mantle, Phil Rizzuto. The Yankees, they can do it all.

"Now you can win a game, maybe a couple, on the breaks or someone's fool error. A ball can hit a pebble, it's been known to happen. But over a full season, see—"

"Seth is right," the self-educated man says. He is small, like Seth, and his gaze continually roves, looking first to John, then Sut, now Seth and back again and all the time plucking at his chin as if pulling at a beard. "There are accidental moments, random events on the diamond. No one can claim—or indeed! even hope for!—a perfect system.

"But your game is so close, as close as we may approach. The rules, Seth. The rules set out the game and determine the fundamentals. There are many motions in your game, many levels and unconscious artful moments. What gives them direction, impetus, flow? They all spring from the rules, of course." He looks at the ballplayers and smiles. They are old friends in five minutes.

"I have watched teams at play, all levels from sandlot to the highest professionals, read the books and the newspapers and talked with my friends in late bars for hours. But this is the first opportunity I've had to talk with actual ballplayers."

Macy smiles. "Just ask. We'll set you straight."

"Many questions." The man smiles broadly; the gum-chewing rubes in sport shirts take on Delphic proportions. "You start with the rules, of course. What would the game be without the rules? Children on corner lots without direction, idle and ignorant men lost in innocent time. A situation we must avoid.

"The rules, then." He looks around the table. The players smile and the self-educated man laughs. "Of course," he continues, "the rules do nor create the action, the action itself is paramount, men with a ball. But the rules formalize the game, give a structure that will be passed on, a union between generations, a direction to the flow.

"How do you get from first to home? These are the verities. Ah...If you move the base five or ten feet in either direction, John, would the game change?"

The self-educated man looks closely at John as if he expects an answer. John moves in his chair, picks up his beer. Before he can speak, the man is explaining to him. "No, John, the plays would be the same always. We are playing baseball, not physics. The players would unconsciously adapt. The structure can be altered, it will hold them—and will always hold them—perfectly in balance."

He looks around the table. No one moves. The players expected him to ask for autographs and here he is tearing their universe apart.

"And the game is all in the rules. How they will be read, who will do the interpreting. A team that wins, a winning strategy is best and that style will be copied, their interpretations will be writ until a new style in a new baseball generation evolves, replaces the old, is triumphant on the playing field and vanquishes the champions of old. A new winning strategy is born from the dust of the old.

"Baseball always changes yet baseball never changes." The self-educated man gestures broadly, opens up exciting new spaces in the bar and, with a shrug, just as suddenly collapses them. His arguments shimmer, he sees them as things of real beauty.

"Look closely now. Do you play the same game as Ruth? As Cobb? Changes in approach, inflection, ways of thinking. In the earliest rules, Seth, you had to score twenty-one runs to win—"

"What! What! This is baseball, man," Seth screams. His voice is tiny. "We've been playing this game forever!"

"I'll grant you, yes, Seth, the rules themselves rarely change. But it's the game that comes from those rules, the styles of play, the players themselves. Men play, they read the rules subjectively, they adapt the smaller parts of the game to their individual talents and specialize. A man is a shortstop—he can play best only in this space on the diamond. More than that, he hits for a low average but he compensates with his superior fielding. Past that, he can hit more consistently with the bases empty, more poorly in clutch situations. He is a strong fielder on certain balls, to his right, say, and weak on others. He can run the bases well or just barely. His arm is weak or strong. He has baseball knowledge or brute strength. He will adapt to the game, in this way help to shape the game—"

"Naw. Hey, see, it's like this—"

"No," the man waves. "But take the great ones, gentlemen, and this is where the proof of your game does lie. The great ones are *pre*consciously great. They will prevail no matter what the structure, the interpretations, the level of competition.

"And there are the precious few, your great Ruthian heroes, who will create. They will adapt the game to themselves. These are the rare ones.

Others can at best only bend the rules. The individual creates his style and the manager molds his team.

"No player is the game. No one, not even Ruth, has been the player for all seasons. The field is open, gentlemen. The prospects are unlimited. What can you do?" He spreads his arms wide. He wants to take them all in, to share his joy and understanding.

"Play the game." Macy cuts in with a wave. Ballplayers play ball, he has the knowledge. "That's how you do it, dammit, not any monkeying around with rules or, hey, structures, not with something like baseball that's perfect as she stands. Just go get yourself out on the field."

"No, Seth, that's not the point." The man signals for another round and smiles. "The game is always evolving toward perfection, don't you see. Every year we move closer to understanding all that man is capable of. Each year there are new players, a new season, records to be broken and legends to be created. Could you imagine a baseball year with *no* broken records? The poverty of that moment!

"You can see how the game itself naturally selects the best of available options. The lively ball, when Ruth took over the game. The pitcher's mound, raised or lowered. And what now might be coming, new interpretations, fresh applications of the rules?" He pauses and smiles again. The self-educated man loves to reason with people. He sees the lines of his argument clear as any box score.

"You have to understand, and this is basic to all that I am saying, once you have set the rules and played that first game, every game that follows is variation, another theme from the same melody, a search for the perfection of that melody.

"And what we can do with that! The infinite possibilities! There is real beauty in your game today, but what could be! The shapes of things to come. Where the style itself tells a story: '…they show, the ancient gods, not through words but deeds, the limits of mortal—'"

"Well!" Says Bunyan. The booth is tight and uncomfortable. He wants out. "How about that. Slade an immortal. Never thought I'd see the day."

Macy turns around. "You're talking nonsense, Bunyan. Straight flat-out nonsense." He sits forward, holds his beer tight in both hands. "What do you think, Sut. About time we was getting out of here."

"No. I'm sorry, no, stay longer." The man pleads. His voice is soft but it fills the bar. "We have so much to discuss. The game, the game as it is, as it could be. Players arrayed against one another in greatest intensity. Please—let me tell you a story."

Macy and Bunyan are up but Sut is listening.

"About the game—the game. Build all you want onto that simple structure. And a man does, it can't be helped. Sut, you love the game and want to know all of it, explain every detail and nuance so that you would love it all the more, you build, build but it gives way, Sut."

Sut grins weakly, shakes his head, hey, no, not really...

"You play a game and win or lose and wonder later just what the game was, the linescore you see in the morning papers, a tick to one side or the other in the standings, two hours out in the hot sun. The game, gentlemen. Your perceptions, the fans, sportswriters, other millions with but the most fleeting impressions. The game may be no more than an office pool in the World Series or it may be the grandest, all-consuming dream of a frustrated fan—or it may be just a game. But always the game is there."

"Damn right," Macy mutters, poisonous as a snake. The juke box sings. Seth lights a cigaret.

"There are reasons, deep-seated reasons we rail against change or the image of change, safety in the game's old knowledge, timeless ritual in the very lack of novelty and the ceremony, the casual elaborate ceremony. John, Seth, you must stay—. Well. But Sut, you'll listen.

"You play the game, so many times you have hit the ball and run the bases, first, second, third, home, you know the patterns, follow the ball, the four bases in line with the corners of the globe, order and consciousness reflected inward and outward, strength in the game, all will come to rest.

"The game changes, Sut. Always changing. There are men who do not want you to know this. If you look closely—there is the secret, Sut, the one small thing they never want to tell you. Rather, they say: 'Baseball never changes.' That story is useful to them. Baseball, the game, solid, impervious, a constant they can point to. 'See, as the game never changes, these things too are invariable,' they say.

"And a man wants to see the structure—any structure. You want to see the shape and size of the game this easily, a constant. But no, it always changes, all the truth of it is flux and chaos, how are we to accept this, the game changes, over and again…

"See, Sut, today you know the players, the teams, your own league, the individual and team styles, how the umpires call them. You can understand the macrocosm through the micro, any one player, that individual over any short span of games, a series or doubleheader, see how he might get hot or slump, might stay in the slump all season and wash out, gone forever. The kid up from the farm can bloom, become a terror at the plate and a tiger in the field, spark the entire team and alter the destiny that seemed inevitable, the miracle rookie.

"Or he can fail in the clutch, his fault or not. He can drive the ball over four hundred feet only to have it taken in at the wall, or watch helplessly as a pop single falls weakly just in front of him, takes a bad bounce and decides a crucial game.

"A new manager or a new star and the team's play may change. A man can watch the game and he won't see these things all at once, they are wonderful and gradual, but if a man is aware he can perceive in small doses single baseball generations, 'I remember when,' nights in the hot-stove league, the game is a stately procession, you can see it quite clearly, the inevitability and even the surprises, the sudden stars and the abrupt fades, even these are fated for once they have passed we can accept them, fit them into our lives and schemes.

"Today on the field the corporate team, powerful Yankees never losing, before that, a baseball generation before, the postwar confusion, warscarred rookies and muscular Slavs, old men and kids during the war, what they could have done if not for the war, and thinking back to further years thin lanternjawed gangling men arms hanging to their knees and buggywhipping blazing fastballs, retiring the potbellied freeswinging power hitters from the days before, earlier summers, the men with brutal bats who took the game from the one-run tacticians, the original game, Wagner and McGraw full of memory sitting along the baseline in the old days, the manager and the great infielder squatting, hunched over a bat, listening but not and gazing across the same diamond, tired hooded eyes and a smile, 'it seems it all happened only yesterday.'

"What would you do if there were no rules, Sut?" The man suddenly leans across the table and looks closely at Sut. He drums his fingers on the table and smiles. "Would you run—would you ever stop running? Would you swing a bat, chase after a bounding ball and know those bounces instinctively? If you caught the ball, what would you do with it?"

"Oh, yeah, I'd keep everything pretty much the same," Sut says. "Getting older," he smiles, "and you like to keep everything on an even keel."

"That's right, Sut," the man says. "Right you are, yes. If I had the power on earth, if any of us did, we would keep things always the way they are. But no. Things change, Sut. We grasp at passing forms and when they are gone we mourn our loss, never knowing, never realizing it is only shadow play, but Sut, nothing can be done. Change…Where does change take us if the world is closed and the change is only repetition, trivial variation?"

The man holds up his hand and smiles self-consciously. "I know, Sut, sometimes I contradict myself. Or sometimes there is nothing there.

Man looks for a view, wants to see the game entire, a unity, spends a life-time in knowledge and seeking, patching up the holes in his framework. But it gapes wide, leaves vast spaces where there should be strengths, all we can ever hope for is a patchwork of understanding held together by faith and inconsistency, don't look at the holes, the spaces past that, there's nothing out there, vast reaches of nothing...

"In the game you want to stay young, stop growing, you won't under-stand because change is death for you. How can an individual adapt, and adapt again, and stay in the game forever? Only the strongest and most primitive. Ruth was an animal. He knew when the weather would change, he could see the stars move. Yet even this man was passed by.

"But you, Sut, you live in one generation only, you see only the futil-ity of change, the crying need for change when there can be no change, when change is all around you, movement in spheres you will never touch, groping, deep in the dark night.

"Is that how it goes, Sut? Nothing..." The man sits back. He signals the bartender for another round but no, the bartender shakes his head, it is past closing time.

"You see how it goes, Sut. The stories from long ago, running in cycles, over and over again, a myth in street clothes, in cleats. We want to see evolution, hope for a better game coming, but in our hearts we know. There will never be another Ruth.

"You forget where it all begins. The same act repeats what the greats and the legends and the minor leaguers and the kids in sandlot games have done for ages, can't you see it, Sut, they won't change, they change again and again, at the bottom there are none, only chaos, only nothing, you can't say it, there has to be something, the Yankees, Babe Ruth.

"Why do men play this game?"

The bar is empty, no one hears him, his voice is too loud and the man is foolish, the ballplayer has put up with him long enough. Sut leaves. The bar is dark, hard blue lights from the beer signs guide his way out, the bartenders stand with crossed arms and watch him leave.

"Tonight's five hundred, Jack. Only one pitcher in all of baseball has ever been there before and I guess you know who that man was!"

Later in the season Jack Slade stands in the dugout, motionless, a difficult man, dark and sure. Long chorus crowds him, friendly as a puppy, smiles and winks, slaps Slade on the shoulder as a fellow athlete would and motions the photographers closer.

"Tonight is the big one, Jack. An important milestone in your pursuit of Cy Young. What does it feel like, pitching your way to baseball immortality?"

Slade doesn't answer. No question. He looks slowly around the dugout, an old familiar place, colorless grey cement grainy as photographs and the bench, long wooden unfinished planks, along the far wall. The lights burn. Slade looks at them flatly. He squeezes the ball in his hand and waits. Long chorus smiles, scuffles loose gravel, laughs weakly. They point pencils, raise stubby black microphones. Cameras flash in Slade's face and he turns away. There's a game tonight.

"Do you feel any added pressure, with this game being so important in the record books?"

Slade picks at his fingernails. He's won the game already, long chorus has awarded it to him. No one could come this far and *lose*, they laugh.

"Are you really going to retire after that last win, Jack? The Tigers could be up there in the race, you know. That would be something to stay for, a real cap to your career. After all..." Long chorus probes, but gently. Deadlines, they say. Get some good quotes. "Uh, with only the one Series to your name, after all these years, and no wins in that one, wouldn't you want the chance to go out as a really big winner?"

One nail digs into the other, patient, methodic, thorough. The cool nights never bother him, he can live without the sun. Slade doesn't move, only his fingers, over and over, white and smooth. He waits. Long chorus needs words, a physical toy to handle. Long chorus must shape every question to the contours of a diamond.

"Don't you remember what happened to Grover Alexander? After he pitched long enough to beat Christy Mathewson's lifetime total, just by one, then they went looking through the old boxscores and found another win for Christy. So that he and Alexander were tied."

Long chorus looks at Slade, smiles weakly. Baseball is their language but they have none of the infielder's grace, no physical balance. Long chorus plods on. "Suppose, say, that Young had been the relief pitcher in a long-ago game and deserved the victory? They'd have to award it to him, like with Alexander and—"

"No. I beat them jokers years ago. I did that way back with St. Louis. They give me the front page headlines."

"But don't you ever think about that? That Young's 511 wins may not be the absolute figure? And what about the future? Just suppose—"

"Cy Young is five hundred and eleven in the record book." No more questions. "Jack Slade will have five hundred tonight and I will be in the record book, five hundred and twelve. For ever."

Slade leaves.

Long chorus waits. Every game they have to ask him the same question, change only the numbers. Sometimes they ask him, "Suppose how Cy Young felt, setting the record so long ago and never knowing where to stop, what number of wins would be the limit, the final win…"

Slade never answers but he knows, tired. Young felt tired.

Long chorus can go to Tyrone Abelmann when they need stories. He's known Slade, played against him for the last twenty years. Abelmann retired once when Slade was still in the National League with the Cards. The Browns hired Tyrone as a coach and when Slade returned to the American League with Detroit, Abelmann went back on the active list.

"That Slade always was a tough nut to figure. You know, hard to believe but playing against and knowing him all this time, not once have

I ever run into the man off the field. Nope, not once. Hardly anyone has. He's not hiding, you understand, it's just that he is never around.

"On the field you think you know him pretty well and that's plenty enough for most folks. Out on the mound there, he's quite a relic. When he pitches, you know you're going to see something. He won't say the first word, no chatter, not to you nor his own teammates, not an insult, not one word. Just stand out there and look at you. Stare. Like he'd stare right through you. Cut you like glass. Most folks can't take it.

"I always stepped out of the box. Haw! That would set him off. See, it's not that he's staring at you, it's the strike zone. He stands out there on the mound and he sees it, like it's a real thing, like the air's a new color or something. Step out and it breaks his concentration." Abelmann smiles and scratches his head. Long chorus sorts through their notes.

"Hardly anyone would do that, though. They'd get caught up when he stared. Always thought he was staring at *you*, like a snake and a bird. Can't break it off. Stand there like a dummy and no wonder the ball comes in so sudden, like out of nowhere.

"He's giving you trouble again, right, no stories?" Abelmann looks closely at each of them. "Well, there's not much you can say. He's winning and he's winning and it looks like the old son a bitch is going to make it.

"Just step out. Hey, tell all the kids that. Put it in your papers. So they learn it early. Slade might be around for a long time to come. Says he'll quit when he beats Young but you don't know, once you're in this game quitting is the last thing you think of.

"But that's the trick and only a few ever learned it. Only a few could ever *do* it. Step out. It's something you have to tell them over and over again but you can just-never-teach!" Tyrone stresses each word. "Hey, you try staring at Slade for too long and everything you learn just goes out the door. Haw!"

Abelmann leans closer, strikes the pose of a conspirator. "Hey—now you want a story, right?" His voice is husky. "Now we got this kid—but I guess you've heard about him. The Cuban Kid Ebony. First of the coloreds we picked up since Veeck left. Hey, that man would a had the whole team colored! Haw! But that crew's out, we cleaned house and now the Ebony's the only one a them we got now. Found him down in Cuba, I guess. Hitting cocoanuts with a broom handle, some such story. Well, House hasn't played him yet. The Kid's good. I'm not second-guessing, you understand. I'm just a coach, see, I don't run the team. But you know we're just sitting still in the standings. Well!

"I've been working with him, you know, a little extra help, taking a look at what this kid can do. The thing is, though, you can't tell the kid anything. He won't listen. But there's a whole lot of ballplayers like that. Four hundred or so! Haw!

"I've been working on his stance." Abelmann sits back, looks across the diamond. One player, deep in the outfield, lazily chases fly balls. "He takes a real sweet cut, he's got a natural swing, and I think, I *really* think, he's going to do great things for the team. Some day. If he'll only listen, let me straighten him out, I think he'll be one fine player. You know, there are a few things in this world you just gotta learn. You aren't born with all the knowledge.

"Doesn't say much, either. Kind of a strange one."

Homer House is the Brown's manager and he has nothing to say to long chorus. He can't play the Kid or put him in the game. There are certain principles, House says. A way to look at things. "The team's coming along," he'll say. "Anyone will have to work their way into the lineup. We're solid in the outfield, we have good players off the bench."

One game early in the year, weeks ago, a tight game, the Browns trail by a run in a game they might win. Hunter bounces out to open the ninth but the next batter singles, the tying run is on base and House sends in a pinch-hitter. He swings a fistful of bats slowly, listening closely to House and nodding as the excited manager pokes and prods him. House points at the enemy pitcher once again, spits the other way and hurries into the dugout. He points at Cuban Kid Ebony, talks rapid and nervous, twisting his pencil and figuring the game.

"Listen to me close now, I'm having Diering up there bunting. We'll sacrifice the runner to second, scoring position, see, that will make it two out and then you're up to bat. Break you in damn quick. It'll all be up to you to drive the run in.

"You've got the hammer, kid."

Ebony looks at him. House is crazy. Ebony watches Diering at bat. He squares away and nods at the pitcher, as if at a signal, and on the pitch he pulls his bat quickly back when the infield jumps in, takes a full cut and snaps the ball past the shortstop, a punch single to left that sends the runner to third.

House is laughing, way back on the bench, pointing at Ebony. "Thought I was going to leave it up to *you*! Crazy, kid, you think I'm crazy?" Laughing, laughing. "Shit, you that's never played but some half-ass Caribee league, think I'd put you up there in the Bigs with a game on the line? A real damn major league game? Crazy, kid. Get your ass back on the bench."

The Kid sits on the bench silently. He waits through the spring, the steamy days of early summer. In pre-game practice the Browns stand around and watch *him*. The Kid hits, runs, leaps and catches long arcing fly balls hanging suspended against the distant fence, pulls the ball back to the playing field; a home run is only a long out against the Kid. He throws the ball like a bolt and all the time his expression never changes.

Some days he wears sun glasses, not only on the field but in the dugout and the locker room. He wears them at batting practice. They wonder why, sitting on the bench and laughing. They don't care. They hate him. He never speaks.

The Kid wears an old medallion with a motto no one could read: *Time Jesum transeuntum et non revertentum.* He is always the last to leave the locker room. When he arrives no one notices him. He appears on the field dressed and warmed up. When he leaves the ballpark no one sees where he goes, underground, invisible.

Another time. He keeps no myths, all his stories are told in the present and moving, moving. When he wakes in the morning it is as if he had never slept. He keeps everything to himself, even the small magic of his name.

House and Abelmann sit on the bench and talk about him back and forth. Abelmann wants the Kid to play. House won't say. He looks at the other coaches, mumbles a few words to one player, laughs with another old vet. But House leaves the Kid on the bench. They all know the Kid might play if he smiled, laughed and danced, shined a few shoes and spat watermelon seeds into gleaming polished spittoons. The spittoons are empty. Tonight the Tigers are beating them. Slade pitches, relentless, a small machine that will never quit.

"This is his big night," Abelmann says. "Five hundred."

House paces in the dugout. Slade retires another batter. Abelmann coughs. House stops. He looks at the Kid. House blinks and rubs at his water-blue sad eyes. "Let's see what you can do, Kid."

Cuban Kid Ebony looks at House. He knows this time it is for real. He stands slowly, picks up a pair of bats and walks huge and slow to the plate. He swings the bats over his head and tosses one away. He digs in. The bleachers explode. Slade stares. Across the diamond they recognize one another. The first pitch puts the Kid flat on his back.

"This is the Bigs, kid," the catcher says as he tosses the ball back to Slade.

Cuban Kid Ebony digs in again. He looks at the scoreboard far away in the outfield. Two out. Last inning. He crowds the strike zone. Slade pitches and the Kid goes down again. Ebony stands, dusts his pants, digs in again. Slade grins—his mouth curls. He winds, fires, the ball cuts the outside corner low—and Ebony moves, his bat twitches, slices the air and crack-sudden!—the ball shoots into space, a clothesline shot deep to right, a beautiful descent and the ball rolls far away into the outfield, the Kid is off and running hard past first and into second, sprints for third base, arms pumping hands reaching and grabbing at the wind, the outfielder so far away chases the ball down, whirls firing to third, a good clean throw, one bounce but a full stride behind the runner—Cuban Kid Ebony slides hard, hard and at the bag, the fielder sweeps the ball in and tags, together they turn to the umpire, frozen in tableau, the ball against the runner's hip, the Kid in sliding posture, the umpire massive in blue staring hard and level into the runner's eyes, he looking back steadily not betraying a thing...

The dust settles. The ballpark is silent as night. Slowly the umpire smiles and slower yet he draws his thumb up, then back, whispers softly, as if to a lover, "You're out, kid."

Time passes: later in the summer the Senators come to St Louis, City of Brass. Everything is the same.

"Tonight," Macy says, feverish and dancing, "tonight's the night. You might think it's all over and done with, gentlemen, but you're sad mistaken. Tonight it all comes together."

Their ballgames are swift, immediate, practiced, a game they all know. Summer wears on them, each game is a collection of incidents, a compilation of numbers changing in tiny increments, random moments caught in memory then forgotten: the Senators are seventh, eighth, up to sixth place, down again, the Senators have no strengths, over the long summer they are sapped, losing, unwilling.

"You boys be on your best in the game this afternoon, because I'm telling you," Macy goes on, "this isn't any of your ordinary games. No, today we are playing a special and extra-ordinary game! One of your highlights in history. Today because Mister Senator Joe McCarthy is going to be in the audience!"

The players are silent. They look at Seth. He smiles, kicks his feet and shuffles through a small dance. He has a private line, a sixth sense that tells him these things. He explains it, taps his chest, "All part of the Loyal American Underground, you know, we keep in touch. And best is, we're all going to see the man, live, real, the man in the flesh. Because, see, after the game the man is springing for a dinner party. A whole party, just for us and some of your bigwigs in town. A dinner and then, hey, a speech after. A speech from the man himself. Everything, soup to nuts. The whole story.

"Hey," Seth smiles, "he's a Senator too, right? See?"

"Just like televison—"

"*Better* than television," says Hardy.

"But do we get the party win or lose, Seth?" says Bunyan. "If we blow the game, that would make kind of a sore spot on your American history, wouldn't it?"

"You're talking nonsense, Bunyan. Straight flat-out nonsense. We're going out there to show them something. Remember, the Brownies don't know McCarthy is here. They won't get none of the benefit."

"But there's the Hearings, Seth. Doesn't he have to stay back in D.C. for those? If he's not there to be the star—"

Seth waves his hand. "No, no, he's just taking the long weekend off and stopping by here to cheer us on. He's a fan, they're all fans. And he's seeing some of the fat cats, too, get a little bankroll to keep the cause going. The deal is, he's headed back to Wisconsin. Back to home base. Some of the locals there, reds or something, are starting up a phony recall campaign and the man has to go settle them down."

"So we get all the benefit—"

"Soup to nuts, like I say. Right after the game the bus is going to take us over to his hotel. Reservations, a private room, everything."

Sudden excitement on the field! Bunyan tags the ball, wood sings and heads snap, the ball carries deep, deep, but foul by feet, bounces through the stands away from anxious crowds, out of the game.

Maybe we'll get to the pitcher early. Knock him out. McCarthy would like that. Right up his alley. Sut smiles and leans back on the bench. All we have to do is pick up the pace here, we're behind in the standings but not that far, get a few wins, we can be back on the track. Work up to sixth place, fifth, fourth—the first division!

I wonder where McCarthy is sitting. You'd think there would be flags up, something, signs pointing him out. Television cameras. Ike had the whole ballpark decorated. But that was for the game, too, for Opening Day, way back when.

But today. Today we've got a game. We win or lose. All right. Down to it. Hey, Ralph might pinch-hit me yet, yes, let's check out that pitcher, get into the game! Sut leans forward.

The pitcher is tall and thin, an anonymous man on the mound, hiding behind his glove and fidgeting. He pitches again—Bunyan drives the ball, swift as a hammer, solid base hit to right! Sut jumps and the bench is up, cheering and yelling, Catfish ambles up to the plate with two down and crowds in close at the plate, dares the pitcher, laughs, the game moves, every player is caught up, everything in motion, the Catfish measures and swings mightily and each time he might connect! but no, three strikes you're out, he stands at home plate while the Senators take the field.

Ralph points to Bartlett on the bench. "Don't embarrass me, son." The Catfish waits at the plate for someone to bring him his glove. Bartlett waves to him as he runs deep into left field. Sut leans back on the bench.

"Boy, that's going to be some show tonight, Sut." Catfish Masaryk plods into the dugout. He is big, big and strong, a slow monster at the plate. He swings and usually misses, but when he connects! Other players stand around and watch. This time he missed. Ralph sits at the other end of the dugout, planning and plotting his own game, the game on the field a poor reflection. "You're going to go see him, aren't you?"

"The whole team is. I think we have to. Hey, now, that wasn't fair of Ralph to pull the hook on you so soon." Outfielders too have their guild, pride and craft. An insult to one...The batter pops the ball, a long fly, deep and high to left, Bartlett backpedaling snaps the ball out of the air with one hand.

"A play like that, Sut," Masaryk smiles and laughs, slaps his hands together, rough and worn hands, "makes old Ralph look like a genius. Now I been *hit* by balls like that!" Masaryk laughs, he claps his hands roughly again and shouts at the team on the field. The play's the thing, the game is a pleasure. In the locker room he listens to the game while he showers. "Hey," he laughs, "go for the fences if they put you in. Go for the long ball, that's what the fans want."

"Right."

"You can believe it, Sut. Give them a show and you'll be driving a Caddy too." And the Catfish does. He ambles away down the bench. Six years ago he hit forty out for the Phillies and bought his Cadillac brand new. Six years later it shines spotless, hard and glossy in the afternoon sun. Sut watches the field.

There's a sweetheart. Sut wanders through the stands, watches the fans as they watch the game. Bunyan when he's on the bench likes to talk and laugh, make up a joke or a story about the women. That's fun. Like that one there, she's staring right at me. But she's black. What Bunyan could think of...I wish I could make up stories like that. Right away, a funny story out of nowhere. The blonde over there, what Bunyan would say. Something funny.

There's lots of funny things about this guy at bat. The kid, the Ebony. Everyone jokes about him but no one can figure him out. There's never anything about him in the papers. But he damn sure knows what he is doing out there.

Lear spits. He catches a few drops and rubs them into the ball. He stands in the middle of the diamond, watched by the fans, the players and managers, the umpires. Lear puts his fingers to his mouth and spits again, drools temptingly, wets the ball until it oozes. The umpire watches. Lear smiles. He rocks back, throws, the ball hurries to the plate then drops amazingly, rolls off an invisible table just in front of the Kid. The Kid swings, twists his wrists dramatically and chases the ball, but only taps it, one dusty bounce back to Lear and he grabs the ball and holds it confidently, ball in his glove and hands on his hips, watches the Kid run fruitlessly to first before he tosses the ball to Bunyan. John reaches out and tags the Kid.

"You're out," he says, and the umpire screams agreement.

Lear has taken control. The Senators are barely scrambling for fifth, sixth place but Lear is having a fine season, Lear has arrived this season, in a class with Wynn and Ford as the record book will testify. Sam is way past the Senators but stuck with them.

Lear sets the tempo, controls time in the timeless game. An inning is three batters, an hour, a few minutes; one pitch is the game, one pitch is the smallest part of the game. Lear sets up false rhythms and expectations with each batter, has him guessing when Lear is playing percents, swinging for the expected pitch when Lear goes against the book. Fastball, curve, slider, same motion, change-up, one pitch looks much like another until the last possible split-second when the ball will drop suddenly, break or rise like an apparition.

Lear is a student of wind pressure, the regular atmospherics, dynamics, physics, the higher and lower mathematics, a touch of hydraulics. Lear grows older learning the game, evolves himself as they all did beginning with the fastball, blazing, a strong-arm kid out of nowhere, then learning the curve ball, control, an easy underhand barrel-hoop curve like the first in the game and later overhand, his own distinctive breaking ball, as personal as a fingerprint. As time and age advance the pitcher experiments: a changeup, first a slow-pitch relying on crude deception, now illusion and finally a genuine reverse english. Other tricks, new grips, slider, knuckleball, a forbidden spitter, a thousand tangents and possibilities, roads taken or not, Lear arrives, a dozen different pitches at his control, the newest, the best of his craft.

Until one night the kid with the fastball, the blazing rookie with nothing but speed, primitive throwback, a caveman on the mound, knocks off Lear in Cleveland. Time stops, marches backward. Lear loses again in his next game but recovers his rhythm, gets back in touch on the mound and pitches.

Sut watches. Lear is damn good this year. Better, every time out, better than any season before. But why that should be…Sut can see the motions, the same moves from Day One, maybe a little more skill, the breaks falling Lear's way now, this season he's ahead of the game but why that is, Sut will never know.

The two Brownie batters after Ebony are no mystery. The teams change round. Bunyan slumps on the bench, sweating and cursing, an honest working man at his job.

"Jesus Christ, Sut. Be glad you don't know what it's like out there. Summer in St. Louis, whoever in the hell invented it ought to be shot. This is no damn *game*, Sut. You have to be nuts to be out there playing."

"You get a good view of the game."

"Hey, right." He smiles. "Lear's got them under his thumb today, boy. I've got nothing to do but play catch with Jonathan and Hardy. Not a tough chance all afternoon, hardly any baserunners at all. But hotter than hell, Sut. Playing in an oven out there. What I wouldn't give for a cold damn beer right now. Out there in the bullpen they've got some, I'm sure."

"Got plenty of good water here, free for the asking. Get a drink and let's sit here and watch the stands. Plenty of people out today, some pretty strange ones too. You know. Hey, take a look."

Bunyan waves at Sut, laughs, and moves down the bench to the water cooler. He takes a long drink, then sits in the distance beside Keyser.

I might get to bat around the eighth. Sut bounces his bat against the cement floor. If the game's still close Ralph might take Bartlett out, or even Lear. Maybe Cott. Or he might not. That darky again, still looking at me. If I was playing—I remember back in Appleton. My first year in the pros. Getting paid to play, hey, imagine that! There was that girl, sat in the same box seat two or three nights a week. One night I finally did talk to her and then the team went on the road and then they called me up to Savannah before we got back. Appleton—never was too sure just where that town was.

If I was playing regular, you never know. Anything could happen. I could find the groove, get into it, wouldn't matter who was pitching or what they threw me. Just got to get into the groove.

Jonathan picks up his tiny bat and hurries to the plate but Ralph is up and yelling, pointing at Sut and then Turle. "I want you up there at bat, McCaslin. Show us what you're getting paid for. Loosen up, you Turle. You're at short next inning. And when McCaslin gets on base, you're running for him." Ralph smiles. "Got it? Get it!"

Sut looks at the scoreboard. Me? What the hell. We're up by a run, we've got Lear out there. Ralph ought not to shake things up so early. There's an order to this game. Everything's fine as she stands, no, I'll bat later. Sut smiles. Ralph nods at him then points. The umpire scribbles on his scorecard. Out in the crowd she looks at him.

All right. I'm up there swinging. I can do it. Then Turle will come in and the ball game will be over. I could run across the field. Through the game and past it all, pick her up and run away. Don't look at me.

Sut loosens up with the bat and walks to the plate. Bunyan smiles and mimics a home-run stroke. Ralph points to him again.

Sut stands in. His bat feels good, he is familiar with it. The best bat he ever owned was the one he made himself years ago. Back in high school he had found a hell of a piece of wood in an old lightning-struck tree and lathed and carved on it for hours. Then it cracked during the state tourney. Now he buys Ted Williams models from the Louisville people.

The pitcher fires and the ball is a bullet, flat and honest. Sut swings and everything is right, the bat drives through the ball, a carpenter's perfect eye, the ball flies to the wall, hits high and bounces away from the fielder, Sut is in the game with a pinch-double. He smiles when Turle comes out to replace him and laughs at the smallest joke.

Ebony takes the Browns' last at-bat, comes to the plate with two down and nobody on. Lear wills the game done. The Senators have gone ahead three-one. But Ebony walks on four pitches and the tying run ambles to the plate. Ebony jogs to first. He looks at Lear as he runs down the baseline, or he looks at Bunyan, Macy, or none of them. He stands on the bag. Cott trots out to the mound.

Macy watches the Kid. The Kid leans, Macy leans with him. I will have to back up the throw if our boy here tries to steal. Keep an eye on him but you can't never tell. The Book says you're not going with two out and you needing two runs, the Book says you're not running with power at the plate. But you can't tell nothing about these coloreds, they got their own idea of the game, hey, he might take off and run straight across the diamond—there he goes!

The Kid is off on the pitch, Lear with a full windup ignores the runner, the Kid flies, dashes and grabs the air, great handfuls, Cott jumps up with the ball and fires across the field—

Fires late and so high. Macy leaps and grabs the ball far behind the bag—the Kid slides and stands again in the same motion, ready to fly down to third if the ball gets through. Macy pulls the ball quickly out of his glove and fakes a throw to Turle. Ebony doesn't move. Macy holds the ball higher, shows it off like a jewel. He tosses the ball back to Lear. Ebony preens, struts on the bag without moving.

Goddam. The Browns are beating us. The Browns are beating us with blacks. Something has got to happen. We have got to get this situation under control.

The Kid smiles at Seth, rare and brief without a word.

Lear stands on the mound and pounds the ball into his glove. Damn, Lear did it. Lear picks up the rosin bag and dramatically kicks it across the infield, he thinks to himself. The umpire stops the game and points to the bag. Turle picks it up and walks to the mound, hands it to Lear and whispers, jokes. Ralph starts out of the dugout but stops, turns back without a sign. Lear will get him.

Lear throws at the batter's head. Macy makes a move toward second, Turle fakes motion, Ebony is back in time. Lear watches. He fires the next pitch, neck-high, close. Macy and Turle both jump, Cott bluffs a throw, the Kid is back. Lear pitches again. Macy doesn't move, Turle pounds his glove and looks but holds. The Kid has a lead—he jumps, stops. Ball three. Ralph starts out of the dugout again but before he can call time Lear spins around and fires the ball to sneaky Apollo, streaking in from center field, Turle blocks the Kid off base and Apollo makes the tag, the ball game is over, Lear over the Browns, three-one.

"It's good to get out of Washington and back to the United States—"

The familiar voice, the same voice, the voice they've always known, syrup and snake oil, Hey!, they all say and turn to one another, Sut looks at Bunyan and even John is smiling, all right! This is the man come to speak with just us! Give us the true facts and the inside story and yes, he's here, he's real, no mistaking this one, a man from the primitive world of men; he grips the podium in huge hairy paws as he wrestles with the speech, he charms, pleases and badgers them, he tramples poor ideas wrapped in words, smashes them flat with himself as the instrument, a cudgel, and he convinces them all with his brutal victory. The team, coaches and players, traveling secretary and trainer, losers all, follow heady words to victory. Tonight in a crystal dream everything changes, their man is here, in the flesh, a crude deliverance, real as the game they just played, the hits and runs they scored, the sunlight—

"As I am certain all you gentlemen realize—" He smiles and reaches out to them, takes them all in with one primitive human move "—the irresponsible left-leaning elements of our free press have been attacking me, moving against me in a vain attempt to destroy our Hearings, turn them into a circus, distract our nation's attention! from the real purposes and dangers.

"The issue is clearly drawn, it has been deliberately! drawn!, the men in power have seen to that, my friends…"

Tonight they deal in certainties, a hard surface to the world, a solid thing, solid and real as a ball, definite limits and definite meanings, what the world tells them is what the world means and they wait, listening for the word.

"What do they wish, gentlemen? To destroy us? To enslave us? To make this grand country their own? The great European wars have reduced them to rubble. There is nothing else that remains, other men dream of possessing what we possess.

"A great and proud country, the richest land, the greatest country in the history! of our planet, rich and beautiful, bounteous, the fruits of the land, my friends, the streams and forests and mountains, rich and beautiful and true…Where have we gone? Have we done some great wrong, that we must now stand on the brink of disaster? Why do we face nuclear wrath and a Russian master?

"That's what I like about this game," the senator tells the Senators. He leans forward on the podium and joins them, grins and winks, leads them to hellfire and brimstone then pulls them back from the abyss. He laughs and rubs his belly, laughs again, laughs. "You damn well win or lose and you know it, exactly, everyone in the ballpark knows it, look up at the scoreboard and it's all laid out for you, look at your scorecard and you know exactly how things went, who is to fault and, of course, you know *this*, gentlemen, the best team is going to win. We have that team, gentlemen. *Why are we losing!*"

He strikes like a hammer. They look at one another. Why?

"Twenty years of treason…Twenty one. Count as high as you wish, my friends. For tonight…Remember our land, our forests, the grand permanence of our rivers and mountains and the greatness of our people. Remember all of this, my friends.

"The Nation, our Nation is but a passing shape against the land, a Nation born of man, a living thing, awkward and mortal, tramping in innocence and ignorance, all of it man's, remember this my friends: all of their talk changes none of this, all the words, all the nightdream structures and hallucinations of government they would ever set up, all must be lies! my friends and you must know this, forces are at work, the world of cruel nature is upon us, the primitive force of the atom threatens to return us to dust…"

McCarthy pauses, he fades in and out of view like a television, a knob out of kilter yet revealing in its juxtapositions. Hardy steps up and fine-tunes and the senator is back in focus.

"Remember, remember, days gone by to which we shall return. Days without fear, nights cool for dreamless sleep. A ballgame's what you want, hold that leather ball in your hand, swing the bat, a ballgame, a real contest between shapes and forces we can see, tangibles, men and objects in motion, the freedom to follow a bouncing ball."

McCarthy pauses and stares at them. The air is so thick and no one breathes.

"There have been threats before! So many have envied our great land, desired to have us fail, destroyed, they wished to grab with clumsy hands and stumble through the gates of Eden. Europe lies wasted, the Old World in dreams, our young land would become their ancient earthly battlefield, international bankers and their monetary conspiracies, yes, these are well known to us…" His eyes flash; a golden gleam shoots quickly across the room. "Secret and most systematic means have been adopted and pursued, with zeal and activity, by wicked artful men in foreign countries, to undermine the foundations of Christian America, to overthrow our altars and deprive the world of our benign society…"

No one moves. The thing is *that* close. They can't pause to think, action is needed, a course must be set and charted, while on the podium force gathers, warm and grasping, visceral. He looks around the room. "There is a war, and no doubt of that, my friends. A war which we, gentlemen, have been losing. We stand on the edge, my friends, pursued and hounded by these shapes and hatreds, driven to a crisis. There is no remote possibility! of this war ending in other than our complete victory or flaming atomic death for this world's civilization!"

It's that clear. Sut can see it.

"The enemy is totally evil, totally unappeasable, a creature of our nighttime. He must be totally destroyed."

Every word sings true. Sut is entranced and totally bemused. He sits on the edge of his seat, holds on tight, he can't slip, he sees atom bombs falling, immense black cylinders dropping out of the clear blue skies, ticking ominously, then swelling thunder, a red flash and a mushrooming cloud covering the whole east coast while diplomats in top hats and fat bankers rub their hands.

"*Why are we losing*! Victims to conspiracy, gentlemen, the conspiracy, history no longer the reflection of man but the tool of men in high places, communists and aristocrats working to the same ends, determined each in his own way to take from us all that we have, reduce us, take the common way and the status quo into their own alien hands, to change our world…A revolutionary dark future, a shapeless nightmare, this I can promise you, we march to the end of the American dream! We are losing and this is *more* than a game!

"They would turn the tide, we must hold fast! The team we are fielding is not America's, no! They play the foreigners' game! We must call them back, send in a pinch-batter for Eisenhower, score a run against these twenty-two! years of treason." McCarthy looks around the room. No one moves. He could be back on televison.

"Sut, uh, McCastin, you often pinch-bat. You know how important that one strong hit can be, how it can turn the tide—" All the team stares at Sut. He is chosen, transfixed. The one man McCarthy picks out of the whole team!

"I am here," McCarthy chants, bringing their attention back to himself, "I am here because I am here, history points to us. Can one imagine a Washington, a Napoleon, born out of their time?" In blinding shifts he changes shapes, becomes and is. "Time points to us, *this*! is the challenge we face today, gentlemen. These communists, these hard men with dark hidden faces are on the march aided by weaklings abroad and traitors at home, this is more than a game," he chants, "more than a game," again "more…"

Macy sits tight, compacted, teetering on the edge of his chair. The man has entranced and snared him again and again, willingly and not, drawn him captive where a rational man would scream free, Seth pulled down and under, caught in swift currents of rhetoric, he grasps, a baseball in his hand, where did that come from it is solid and round, a shape he won't forget, not ever, he squeezes hard and the ball disappears, off balance he slides, Seth slips into private bayous, sails up mossy-veiled rivers toward darkness, absolute quiet darkness, he glances behind and there is the grand conspiracy of man, now a shape hidden like a ghost, moving in forms through everything he knows, a fleeting remembrance or taste, a bare memory of cracks and seams, he would escape from it all, drift away but it follows him, a light in his darkness, shadow in his light, now the things he knew all along fade away: then Eisenhower was never—not even the game—Mantle, Slade, even Ruth—the country, America, everything—nothing but huge foils, metal surfaces revealing nothing, cast in gleaming-dull greys, huge dynamos shaping the destiny of man but, out of the corner of his eye, oozing away 'round corners, glimpsed only fleetingly, bloated slimy pink shapes, unknown brute creatures gone too quickly, jolting the oldest memory. Conspiracy, he says. More, more than that, communists, fascists, Catholics, Masons, reds, blues, brownshirts, village carpenters and statesmen, plowmen and priests on the Nile...Four thousand years of treason.

Around him is force, flashing red lights and ruby-skinned humanoids rushing away, no man will speak to him, harsh tones echo from loudspeakers down hallways, he looks up quickly to see a loud-speaker pointed at him: no release, no where, they all must protect themselves, everything becomes known, he looks around desperately but nowhere to go...Macy curls tightly as a kitten. He dreams. Soon he will wake and things will be as they used to be.

"So what's it mean, Sut?" The street is long, dark and sinister, Sut knew where they were going once but damned if he does now, Bunyan points to darkened windows and empty lots, Sut hears quiet voices and whispers, words just out of reach, without meaning, "and what difference will it make anyway? Tomorrow we've got another game, and well, you know how it goes."

"Right..." Not right. This is the game, hey, John has to know better than that. Tell him that tomorrow anything might...Today nothing. "But John. You've got to think about these things, about what McCarthy said—"

"No such man," Bunyan says. "Never saw him on a diamond. And if he did say anything," John smiles, "I didn't hear it. Just play the game, Sut, that's all you have to know, play the game while you can, a few more years but remember we none of us are ballplayers forever."

"But we are yet. Ralph told me so not a week ago. He said it costs Owner too many bucks to bring up a rookie and drop a vet. 'You know the ropes, kid,' he said. 'That's all we need around here.'"

"And the corn always grows, right, Sut? So you've got nothing to worry about."

"The corn *al*-ways grows. Yes my friend it *does*."

They walk past a dark alleyway and the man joins them, strides out on cue, marches with them in loose lockstep down the street. He is instantly friendly, a stranger they've known for years. Streetlights hide them, streetlights reveal, together the three of them slowly walk the city streets.

"And what about you, John? 'Big John,' they call you, the most dependable one. Am I right?"

Bunyan smiles. "Buy me a drink?"

"Yes—you're the player who hits the ball well in the clutch situations. You save the game when possible, pull the team from the brink of defeat. The anchor of the infield. The heart of the batting order. Yet the team loses—you lose. Each defeat hangs around *your* neck. John—can this be right? Can this be fair?

"Come the end of the year they will total everything up, create a sliding scale, the game's ratings. Joe Collins—yes. Bill Skowron. These men will be your All-Star first basemen. And then there's Bunyan, they say as well, but a little behind, a little short. Maybe if he pushed, tried just a little harder. You hear their voices, John.

"You hit the ball well this season. Men on base ahead of you. A little quicker in the field. Keep it up all season and you can be up there. You might be the one. An empty epiphany, but this could be your year.

"And you play. But, tell me, John, if you did not play first base—would your team have no first baseman?"

"Hey, yeah!" Bunyan laughs. "It's the breaks, you know. But what the hell, they haven't missed a payday yet. Now here's a cocktail lounge. What a deal. There's the place to stop for that drink, obviously."

"One for the road," says Sut. He pulls at the heavy wooden door—open! Only light plywood and paint—Sut stumbles inside. Bright lights, satin plush, rayons gleam like wet-toothed smiles, stark white lights, white and sea-green plastics, absurd planters, hollow noises from everything. Sut walks into the center of the room feeling dirty and rumpled.

"Hey Bruno!" The bar is empty but for Petrarkis, sitting at the shag-rug bar, huddled over a colored drink. He turns to them and waves, slowly. Even relaxed he is worried, concerned, constantly adding up his old numbers and memories.

"John! Sut! Looks like you've had quite a night already. What's up, got time for another round?" He points to the bartender. "Buy me a beer?"

"Where'd your friend go, John?"

"Bruno-poodle." Bunyan stumbles into a stool, knocks it over. "Long night." He picks it up and sits carefully. "What is that crap you're drinking?"

"They serve mixed drinks here, John. Any damn thing you want, booze that tastes like ice cream, or peppermints, all kinds of things you'd never imagine. I tell you, the things you'd never imagine—"

"Are they having a bed check tonight, Poodle?" asks Sut. "Is Ralph keeping curfew again?"

"Keyser's in the lobby, but he's only looking for blood and major bruises. Doing his crossword puzzles. As soon as he's got nine or ten ballplayers safe in bed, enough for a game, he'll pack it in himself. We're free, see, to do anything we want." He smiles and half-lifts his drink, a small toast. "Get one of these, John. They are the damnedest things."

"Bruno-poodle." Bunyan squints, searches the corners of the room. Details are fuzzy, angles bend, pictures in his mind begin to spin. He has questions and wants answers. "What's coming, Bruno? More of the same? What does it all hold?"

The questions are suddenly very important, looming out of grey space, massed threats.

"No, no, John." Bruno smiles and with a wave dismisses them all. The questions shrink to nothing. Bruno sees what's coming in personal terms. "It's not like that at all. Some day we'll get caught up and leave all of this behind. We're good, you know, good enough for sixth, seventh this year and who knows, maybe…"

No, says Bunyan, but he doesn't interrupt. He'll let Bruno ramble on. And Sut will listen to anyone.

"The years will be good to us, John. We've planned for it and have everything prepared, a few more years on the active list playing ball and then—"

"Don't you ever wonder, though, what you'll do when baseball is through with you? What it will be like? Where you'll go when the old men are through with their pampering and the fans done with their idolatry?" Bunyan taps his drink on the bar in a slow rhythm.

"Hey, those big words again." Petrarkis smiles broadly. "You have to come down a few levels if you want to get through to us poor dolts." He winks at Sut.

"Silent Sut here has the solace of his farmlands to fall back on but what do such as we have?"

"Another drink, hey. And I'm buying." Petrarkis waves at the bartender. "Get one of these, John. I'm telling you."

"Seriously."

"Bunyan, damn it, you're a star." Petrarkis is briefly angered. Why can't everyone plan it out? "What the hell do you have to worry about? If you want a farm, go out and buy one. That's how things are. Buy two, feel twice as good." Petrarkis smiles. The jukebox swells with a saxophone and he drums his fingers.

"Besides, I'm not leaving baseball. Not as long as I can help it. It's too good. Half the year off and look at the pension plan. I could be up here for another four or five years, active playing, and that means more than a hundred a month when I'm only sixty. And the more years I get in, the more money I'll pull down. You've got to know the ways of the world."

"Just stay in baseball." Bunyan holds the idea as if it were brand-new, something he had never seen before. "Just hang around."

"Now, John, they told me if I…They told me I could be a coach, after I'm done playing, if I last long enough. They said maybe I could coach, then manage in the low minors for a few years, work my way back up the system—just like when I was a player, see, only now I'll be the one in charge. And some day a big league coach, and later, after that, maybe—"

Petrarkis is bent over the bar again, as he was when they came in, staring into his drink, locked in cages within himself, Chinese puzzles forever reduplicated, smaller and smaller, precise in detail and the smallest exactly like the largest.

"I could have gone running off years ago. Back with Barney Callahan. We had a small dance combo, we were the guts of it, we played around home for a few years, played for beer money around the bars, picked up loose change and women. So Barney went off to New York years ago, just took off, making for himself not one damn cent. Not assured, any-way. Wanted me to go with him. Crazy bastard." He looks at Bunyan. "Stupid bastard."

"Sorry you feel that way—"

"No, no, not you, me, him! Crazy fool Barney probably starved to death or something. Never see him around the ballpark. You'd think he would stop in some time, ask for tickets or a handout.

"No, we'd set up on the stage or in the bars, the two of us and whoever we'd hired for rhythm, we'd play a little country, some Broadway, what-ever was popular. Say, sometimes we'd be playing, try a little variation, new arrangements or something, and we'd drift off, just playing. Like everything would open up, we had music, didn't have a tune or nothing, like there was nothing, no limits, not even thinking about any limits.

"Now I bet he's starving or something. I should try and look him up some time. Try all the flophouses in New York." Petrarkis smiles to him-self. "He was a damn fine fielder, he was. That's how I ran into him. He couldn't hit for shit, would never have made the big time or even the high minors, but he sure could look sweet out there in the field. He's probably laid out in some flophouse now, hocked his music and got nothing coming, assured.

"'Anything for Anybody,' that's what we played. We did play in some damn big dance halls before Barney left. Even tried a little jazz every now and then, the mellow stuff. None of this far out outer space stuff they have now."

Sut smokes. It burns his eyes. He coughs. Sut is tired, dreams briefly, Bruno describes yesterday and it's little words, they march over the table, he describes today, tomorrow, little words keep on marching by...

"I still doodle on the piano a little. Music is a wonderful thing, something you should never let go. But you can't let it run your life, either. You'd get lost in it. I've seen the people get addicted to it like it was dope or something. None of that for me. No pension in music. When Barney's sixty, if he makes it that far, he won't get no secure hundred a month."

"Who the hell is Barney?"

"The name's K.C." He points to an empty stool. Why not. Vaguely Sut wonders where Bruno and John have gone. He wonders where he is as well, but the thought passes. Come this far already, no reason to turn back, and far from certain which direction 'back' would be.

"Like I'm from Kansas City," the man says, "or my names begin with K and C. Something along those lines."

"Well...Are you from Kansas City?"

"No. Who are you?"

"My name's Sut. You might have heard of me. I'm a ballplayer, see."

"Oh!" K.C. straightens himself on the stool. His hands, big and red, tighten around his beer. He shakes his head, thick yellow hair. "So you're a ballplayer."

Sure am, Sut nods.

"A professional. A man of special insight and ability, a genius with a leather pellet, one of a rare group. Out in the fields, name in the papers.

Headlines. An American star. Everything, huh? So which one are you? Mantle? Ford? Billie Mays?"

"No, hey, no, I just play for the Washington Senators. I pinch-hit some, play in the outfield every now and then, wait on the bench for when they need me—"

"You're not Mantle? What is your name, then? Who are you?" K.C. is intent. He stares at Sut, big red-rimmed eyes, slurs a few words but picks up his speech rapidly, voice rising in pitch as he speaks faster.

"I did notice some new names in the headlines last night—didn't read the stories. There's nothing in that. Stories are only half-digested details, points of intersection in a man's life and you'll never get the full story from that. The papers want to pin them together, pile them in dizzying order, random snapshots, that's not the way—it's the names. Read through the newspapers for the names, how they sound can tell you so much, how the man carries himself, where he will go and what he is to us, a finer taste than anything in their gross and ridiculous stories. There is a new name: Krishna Menon. Not in the sports pages, surely, but a soft gentle breeze, messages from the east, hints and meanings we would do well to consider.

"On the other hand: Stalin. A grinding noise. Malenkov. A tin monster unfolding. But Eisenhower, I-sen-*how*-er, Ike! I *like* Ike!" K.C. smiles. He waves and a beer is on the table, bubbling and inviting. Everything he says, Sut must agree with.

"And the names in your game. A man need not watch the individual games, a glance at the lineup cards will suffice. Facts in themselves. Mantle, Ford. Winners, solid and corporate. Other places: Chi!co Carrasquel and Nelliefox. A quick and pleasing double play. Minnie Saturino Orestes Arrieta Armas Minoso—the White Sox may not win, but they certainly do go! And could a name on a diamond inspire more fear than Kluzewski? Frankenstein!"

Sut drinks, a long drink, eager and satisfied. That's right, that's right, baseball is like that, you understand.

"So are you one of the kids?" K.C. stares at Sut, leans forward on the bar, a hulking presence. "One of the new players out of nowhere just up to the big time? Are you the answer, the answer for this year, will you lead your team to new glories?"

"No, no." Sut has to smile. "I been around, played for a few years now. Five years in the Bigs. Even made the made the All-Star team once. Back in the Carolina League."

"The Carolina League. A melodious place, I am certain. Yes. And now you are of the Senators from Washington, D.C. D.C., is that District City? Do they call people from that place D.C.?" He hurries on, doesn't care for an answer. "And there are the Yankees of New York City. You are the ones that always lose, correct? A neat system. You lose so that the Yankees may always win."

"Wait, wait, no, that's not right. That's not the game. We lose a lot, sure, but we always play our best, you've got to know that. It's the talent, it's the breaks—"

"Talent? Pick up a ball, toss it in the air and hit it? Chase the ball down, throw the ball and watch it twist and turn? Talent? A round white ball, a point in space expanded, no more than that, you throw the ball and think control and think even more that *you* are that control? That is your talent? Gravity, acceleration, dynamics of brute force control the ball. You know that, Sut. A curve ball breaks no matter who throws the ball. Simple laws of physics." K.C. smiles. He has proven something.

"No, it's more than that, think of all the fans, thousands of people at every game and everyone watching, what it means to them—"

"What it means? A large question, Sut. The game has order, the game has structure, a slow and ponderous, powerful progression across the diamond, the game's in all of us but..."

"What do you learn from an individual game? There's a problem. Some facts are obvious. Acceleration. Men on the move, men scoring. The simple physics of a thrown ball, the dynamic of a swinging bat.

"Where does it lead? What do we look for as the game progresses in time, does it grow, what do we search for? It is as if we hasten to an end, Sut, desiring in the game—by means of the game—we wish to accelerate progress: long slow dusty afternoons at the ballpark we watch for runners to score, destroy the scoreless vacuum, hit the ball hard, over the fences, score runs, as if runs themselves held meaning or showed true force, an accumulation of power. The game brings these forces together, we move along these lines and wonder where these blind forces might lead us, where we have come to, where we are to go.

"What's going to happen, Sut? Will the game show us? Forces are at work. As you think you control that ball, you think of the forces at work there and in the larger places of the world, and all of them under control, perhaps you imagine fat humming dynamos vibrating under your hand like a kitten purring, all yours, you might imagine, all of it, you stroke and feed, every time they ask for more, produce more, more acceleration, acceleration and growth, more, they demand, you give them more, they demand, more, more...

"Well, Sut."

This man knows things, Sut can see that, this large gentle man sits on his bar stool all night and comes to conclusions, easy and natural, like a farmer knows how to plant or a batter knows hitting. Just like that.

"What it comes down to, not a thing you would know or have any control over, Sut. Blind, random force. You stand out on the field, the wide open field, one man tosses a ball and within reasonable limits that ball could do anything. Another man has a wooden stick, not flat so that he might hit the ball solidly, no, the stick is round. Only the smallest possibility exists of his actually hitting the ball, the random chance of contact so rare, arbitrary, nearly unheard of. And any less than a solid hit, an uncertainty, two round surfaces meeting at great speeds, that ball too might do anything. A man waits for the ball, thinks that because he is aware of habits and patterns, past happenstance, that he can play almost precisely the spot in that vast ballpark where the ball will be hit—"

"They do, right, it's true. The good ones can do all of that," says Sut.

"Do? They do? Who, Sut? The players only follow the game, once the ball is set in motion. The bad bounce, lucky hit or Texas Leaguer, the unexpected. These decide the game. But man won't admit that, men strive to perceive *some* order, create elaborate statistics to prove small points, translate the game to the mundane level of their own lives, but ignore the last fact. It is the random event, Sut, the one glimpse of chaos, rent in the fabric, *that* is what decides each game."

"What? Hey. No," says Sut.

"All that you know, of the game you play, player, or past that, of the night outside or this dark bar, tomorrow or me, what *can* you tell? Random glimpses at best, cracked mirrors, the wrong word and a clumsy motion. You reach—nothing there. Names. The rules. That's right, I see your eyes light up, your mind suddenly clears. The rules." K.C. looks around the bar. He makes large movements with his hands and draws Sut closer.

"When the ball is hit to you, player, how do you react? A moment of blind indecision, a wonderment in your mind until you can lose control and your body takes over—trained? You say it is skill, response and deadly maneuver? A ball hit in the air?" He laughs, coughs, turns away from Sut. "You think that it means a thing? A damn thing?"

Sut did. He smiles. He frowns. He remembers the first fly ball he ever caught, taking a few steps in, a few steps out, opening and then closing his glove, opening it again and finding the ball there, a tiny flower.

"Yes, player, they tell you there are rules, and a course to the game, sweet order in the air. The fans applaud your every move. Such a fair picture! You relax, you seem to be at one with it all, drink in the air, take it all deeply with your senses, the ball is hit and it floats in the air, you relax, fleeting but real impressions of the world flip by, you reach but the landscapes are wrong in a thousand details, a moment out of time, night comes, you relax, sleep, our world is an ocean and down below you can see forces moving like primitive fish—you awaken.

"All the order you wish—what is it built upon, player? Words, names, rules, we pursue them to a tentative unity, but won't look beyond. The pendulum swings back." He takes a letter from his pocket, a letter torn in half, still in its envelope, unopened, unread.

"Even the game at bottom is a mechanical object, an imposition on the nature of nature, measured distances and totaled scores, a machine of order and structure. Men following order. Where is the game, then? A hideaway from chaos? If the game were only a game—

"Player, would you play for free? Would you play for smaller rewards? The admiration of your home town? If there were no newspapers, no statistics, not fame or the structure or a thing for the fans to touch or even fans at all, only your strong right arm, lightning bat, runs scored and games won and games as quickly forgotten, now passed into raw legend, into a different and stately structure, dreams only, not pinned down by *any* numbers, the newspapers, yes, and the way it is player— how do you want it? How will you see it? Later there is nothing left, not anything, the empty end of numbers and newspapers, tramps sleep rolled up in newspapers, laid out like inky corpses in the park, chilly evenings ahead, newspapers blow down the empty streets...

...cats scamper after rats through black alleys, shapes crouch in dark hallways, night breezes wrap around him with a touch of autumn melancholy, he feels so alone, strange, nighttime—it's hours until dawn. He hurries down the streets and pulls his light jacket tight. Above him the cold stars revolve, locked away in a further aether, distant layers of his geocentric world. Things happen, nothing happens, he hurries on.

(Or maybe he's wrong. Maybe it *is* a wide universe, open in every direction where everything spins around nothing, against itself in never-ending never-forming circles, a ballet of order and meaning and structure mocking him, so far away, but damn if they could prove any of it by him unless they put him up there to see the whole works, elevated him or shot him up in one of those outer-space rockets and even then, no, it was a hell of a long way to go and he would no believe it anyway because he thought it not believable.)

Further ahead the night changes. The dark surrounds him like a cave but as he walks on he emerges blinking into a forest of new hard white buildings, night neons, constant motion in the shadows, life in the night. The air excites him; a cool breeze promises motion and surprises. In the night are endless possibilities, chance combinations; his walk down the street reveals to him places he knows from the back of his mind, familiar faces loom and disappear, a new world he had known some time before is returning.

He stops. You can't live at night. It's not natural. A man should be up with first light, in bed at dark.

A woman walks by, an echo of every mystery in the night. He waits on a corner as the stoplight eases through its spectrum. Any moment he might fall, the sky might open and the distant seas part, a pointing hand reveal itself and he would fall, tumble head over heels, down through the years, away…

The moment passes. He is out, late at night, deep in St. Louis, miles and miles from home. Traffic pauses and he crosses the street.

He is hungry. He rubs his stomach. Awfully big to feel so empty. He hurries on down the street. Neon in the night and bare street lamps light his way. Passing an alleyway he notices a vent fan, black and thick with old grease, chopping away behind a mesh cage, delivering the most fascinating greasy odors. This is it, he says. Shelter. He peeks in the tiny window and squints at bright yellow lights, steam rolling out of huge pots, can hear glasses tinkling through the washer and a radio playing and grease popping on the grill. This is the place, he says again.

Out front—"Ed's Good Eats" across the sky in red neon—the door sticks. He stops. They're not closed, are they? Couldn't be. He pushes again—two small tight swinging doors open into a cramped vestibule not much wider than the doors and only square. The inside door is to his right, black and white tiles on the floor and up the walls all the way to the ceiling. He has to push past the open outside door, more trouble than should be, but then, late at night, he glides into soft warm air, a crowded café, buzzing talk.

He smiles. A fat waitress smiles back, a tall grill cook wearing a genuine chef's hat nods to him, slabs of pie grin, waiting to be served. This is a good place, he says. Dishes clatter hello, huge happy overhead fans slice choppily swish! ah-swish! through the thick air saying glad to see you here! He sits at the counter and plays with a menu. The waitress smiles again, early in the morning late at night he points out the dinner special, she sets down a glass of water and dances away.

Sut looks around. The café is brightly lit, full of bright bustling activity. Comfortable, a safe place. Shift workers, night people, folks in booths laughing and calling back and forth while waitresses run to refill cups of coffee, all part of the crowd, Ed's crowd, every good place has a crowd.

Back home in Calvinton, Sut remembers, years back, they would hang out around the service station, late at night, high star-filled nights, soda pop and gin, a pool hall around the corner but on spring nights, all summer long, they stayed outside, sitting on cars, talking. The girls came by and they called and joked, laughed, talked about the high school teams and Sut always smiled, yeah, that's me all right, and they sat in the back seats and talked, what tomorrow or the years might bring. He remembers the night he quit school for good to go play fast semipro where the scouts would be watching, hey, that was a time. Everything would come together, everything would be delivered and from there on out nothing would stop him. Sut was on the way, on the road. Christiana was there. She called herself Kristy-Ann, a younger name, a cheerleader at another school but she knew all about Sut, everyone in the county did. That's where I should have stopped being famous. He smiles. Countywide was far enough.

The waitress is all smiles and she has his meal. Sut digs in. Dripping roast beef, thick mashed potatoes with plenty of gravy—Ed knows how to cook!

Between bites Sut leans forward and looks around. People he knows. A nice comfortable place, warm and thick as the potatoes. Mostly white too. There's a few black folk, mostly working in the back. A few others. One woman near the rear.

Oh! it's her. Sut recognizes the woman immediately. She was in the ballpark today and she is here tonight. Sut is stricken with sudden wonder. He stares at her and forgets who he is staring at.

She looks back to him. She has finished eating. Her dishes are pushed forward, she holds a cigaret in her hand by the very tip, pulls at it quickly then holds it away at arm's length. She is looking at him again. Sut sits back quickly. She smiles. Slow, lips like curtains, her face opens. Different, softer in the dim light than in the ballpark sun. Not as dark. Different.

Sut stands. He looks at her. She is dressed nicely, loose grey skirt, soft red wool-patterned sweater, and still looking at him. Sut waits, mouth hanging open. He pulls it shut and almost smiles. He takes a step. She jumps away, picks up her purse and hurries out. Sut watches her leave. Pop, out the door. The door closes.

Sut stands in the middle of the floor. He is open on all sides, waiting. Arrows might strike him. His meal is on the counter, steaming and warm. The waitress looks at him. She smiles. Will he?

Sut isn't hungry any more. He puts a bill on the counter, waves at the waitress and his other new friends, walks away and heads back to his hotel. The night is over, he says.

On the street he stops. He looks in both directions, off into the night, nothing to be seen at either end. If he goes home to bed, sure enough the sun will rise come morning.

Three blocks later he finds her again. He sees her from behind. Same sweater, same skirt. He knows it is her. Same skin, too. She is huddled over, cupping a cigaret, wants to hide from the breezes in the city-caverns. She can't, the wind puts out another match.

Lucky Sut! He has his Zippo from the war. He walks up beside her, snaps the flint. She accepts the flame, touches his hand lightly to guide it. When the cigaret takes, she looks up smiling and—

"Oh!" she says and leaps away, drops the cigaret and hurries up the block. Sut watches the cigaret. Should he pick it up, he wonders. He leaves it behind and chases after her.

"Howdy." What is he going to say?

"Hello." She stops, turns and looks at him. Sut stares at her. This should be easy, he thinks, but he can't say anything. He looks at her again, measures her as empty images run through his mind. Short, but tall as his wife. She is cute, or something. Exotic. Different. His hands open and close. He grabs at something. Her eyes smile, she smiles and she is talking.

"Don't you know where you are?" but she smiles. "Walking up to a strange woman in a big city like this. What am I supposed to think?"

"Uh, I guess I thought I knew you from some place."

"That's quite a line you've got, Sut." She stops, claps her hand to her mouth and hurries off again down the street. Sut smiles. Something is working out here. He follows after her.

They walk together down Jefferson Street. The night around them is liquid and cool, damp noises relaxing after the long hot day. They cross through deep shadows as she talks. Sut smiles and grunts, listens to a thousand tiny and unimportant details of her life, could as easily be his, she smiles, he listens and they laugh softly. Her name is Ivy, she tells him, Sut smiles, fine, everything's fine with Sut. Tomorrow he has another ball game. Tonight Bunyan will cover for him if necessary, make a fake man-figure with pillows in his bed should Keyser be checking rooms. Not that Ed ever would.

Her apartment—they stop. A duplex, thousands exactly like it throughout the city, a well-kept building, the grass trimmed, the paint new, a single row of flowers in the front. An iron fence, but a short one, half a foot high, runs around the yard.

The steps sag. Up the porch, Sut waits while she sorts in her purse, pulls out her keys and unlocks the door. She fumbles with the latch then pushes open the glass-front door. Venetians softly rattle. "Upstairs," she says quietly.

Sut slips past her and hurries up the narrow stairs. They squeak familiarly, many old friends have walked this way, he follows the railing up to darkness, strong sweet odors of musk and scents guide him, promises. Sut smiles. Anything might happen. Ivy pulls the door tight and slips the lock, then switches on a small light and follows him up.

Sut waits at the top of the stairs, staring at the door. Through here…Nice work. The door is a product, a craft, turned and stained by hand. No machine did this. He turns the handle then stops. A face on the door stares at him, someone he knows, a drawing, sad smile, soft eyes, curly handsome beard and locks, a man he's always known, a small card, a picture of—who?

She stands behind him, close. Sut hurries into her apartment. What more mysteries lie ahead, what is so ordinary and exotic, two new people, their patterns, the door swings shut behind him into a brand-new life, tiny signs and another intimate being, unexplored monsters of the deep…

She moves in the dark, her dark shapes round and exciting, brief reflections from eager streetlights, rolling the two of them together on a sheet she had carefully spread on the floor. Now she lights a match and the room is golden, a cave, every shadow dances when she walks on dancing feet to the fireplace—she turns round to him, smiles, shadows all over, bends down to light the fire—"They were going to plug this up, can you imagine?"—squatting over the young flame like a native, in the dark, the two of them could be anyone anywhere at any time, nude as the light flickering over them, living bodies the only detail, nothing else in the room, an ancient clearing—"but we hardly ever use it."

He grabs for her and they laugh. He touches her softly, more softly than he thought he could, smiling, they explore one another, new desires each time, rolling together and caressing, two of them build toward one, rubbing, pulling and playing, atop and around, friction and animal desires, pushing, pushing, he wants and anticipates, the moment coming there! but (this one moment he feels himself crossing over, aware and sympathetic, small shifts in his earth and he totters, this minute they could belong and he would be here, this minute promises, forever...) he loses her, in the fading firelight they are two sweating animals, in man's smells and moistness, he finishes and rolls off, later he is sad. She lights a cigaret and he lay back watching the smoke dance toward the ceiling and where does it go, he wonders, where does it go, what is so damned wonderful about life when you always regret past moments, but on the diamond a man doesn't anticipate, no expectations or disappointments, only playing.

Sut smiles at the table, waiting while she hurries his breakfast. Everything in the kitchen, everything in the apartment fascinates him. Small details stand out, living colors, clean enamel reds and airy light blues, Ivy's voice dances, snap, crackling! home noises, he watches as she scrapes his eggs cleanly off the griddle and places his breakfast before him, talking all the while, bright and pleasant.

She's been married. Sut doesn't ask. Does she have any children? Sut didn't see any. She holds up one finger and smiles. "Just the one...kid." Daisies grow on the window behind her, white curtains with yellow daisies on bright red checks in the warm sun. "Such a pretty little thing, just starting high school this year, bright and pretty." Sut smiles. Ivy frowns. "Pretty little brat."

"Where is she?" Sut butters his toast, spoons on preserves and works at his breakfast. Eggs, bacon, an orange and toast. He takes a bite of each, then coffee, steaming out of the cup to greet him, eggs to bacon, another slice of orange.

"She'll be back later this morning. You'll have to leave pretty soon."

The table here. Sut chews carefully, swallowing the toast before he drinks more coffee. Nothing fancy, kind of small. If the drop-leaves were up, it would be much bigger. A modern piece like you'd find any-where, chrome-tube legs, checked tablecloth. Patterns exactly like he'd seen in one hotel—whi h one? If you start to forget, forget anything, they say you're too old.

"Last night she was staying with one of her girl friends. But she'll be home around noon. She has summer classes and a little job too. When she's home, I don't want her bothered with folks coming in and out."

Back home the furniture was oak, all painted white, the woodwork was white and all the walls were white, the sideboards scrubbed clean and spotless, cool in the winter when Sut was home, when the house seemed cold and empty. In Ivy's small kitchen colors are everywhere, the bright painted flowers on the tablecloth repeated throughout the room, bright bunches of flowers on the refrigerator, buds on the toaster, apples and pears on the wall. If there were no food on his plate he could live off the decorations. Happy ever after, like a tune in his mind.

"Ivy." He smiles, he has to tell her something. Words, he feels he knows her so well, the one night was years into the past.

"Now, you have a while yet. She won't be back for a couple hours. Don't you have a game today?" Ivy smiles. "You should be gone by then." She looks at him. Sut looks at his plate. "Oh? What were you thinking of, Sut? I live here. So does my daughter. This is our home. I don't want you to think—I have a job, you have work too. You're a ballplayer and you have a game today. I like you, Sut, we'll see each other again. You come through here two or three times a year and then—"

"Suppose I get traded?" Things shouldn't be going like this. He blurts out the first thing that comes to his empty mind.

Ivy laughs, a bright ripple, not mocking. "Who would trade for a .230 hitter? You've been on that team for what, four or five years now, and the rest of the league doesn't know you're alive. You're staying right where you are, Sut."

"Well, well, look at Irv Noren." He doesn't know why he chases the dead end. He has to say something. Logic, that's the clue. "He used to be on our bench, just sitting, then the Yanks pick him up and now he's an All-Star." Sut believes this logical connection. Only natural, in his happy world.

Ivy smiles but doesn't laugh. "All right, trade yourself to the Yankees. Be the all star. You'll still be coming through St. Louis." She sparkles, she shines. "Trade yourself to the Nationals. You'll be through here playing the Cards."

This isn't the question, Sut knows that. He plays with his silverware. He feels old and tired and he can't think, he can't move on the easiest surface, can't talk to her. The clock moves. Every minute hurries him. Soon he will be gone for good—he can't come back, once he does leave Ivy and the apartment will go up in smoke and disappear forever—back to the ball club, sit on the bench, play out the schedule.

"I'm going to leave the team."

Ivy frowns. Here eyes open wide. There. Sut's future is suddenly open, all wide spaces, without shape, form or gravity. Ivy moves to him.

"You're what! You're not!"

Sut sits tight in his chair. If he is honest, he knows his ballplaying is over. No, he says. He might stand on the field again or be signed for another season but every dream is long dead. 'Sut McCaslin, valuable reserve and pinch-hitter.' No more bubble-gum cards, next season the kids will throw the old ones out and that will be the end of it. If he jumps, he has life and controls his destiny. Ivy will take him in, Sut the ballplayer, he'll never have to change. If the ballclub released him, he would sink back to earth, farm the land forever and disappear.

"I'm going to leave the team," he says again. "Jump." Ivy stares at him, leans closer to him, hands on her knees. "I've had enough," he says. "There's nothing there." Sut takes the leap, moves between the two worlds. Some day he can look back and smile. "I don't want—I want to stay here, Ivy. For a while." He can't see her face when she is staring right at him.

"Are you crazy, you out of your head?" She smiles and Sut knows her again, quickly. They will live together for a season or more, he'll always be a ballplayer, and the team—they might be looking for me, worrying, Ralph on the phone to the newspapers, hospitals, calling up the police. "I know you're crazy," she says, "walking up to a strange nigger-woman just like you would..."

Sut wins. Listen to what she calls herself! He smiles, he can't help it, that easy! Once he was a ballplayer, traveled with the team, knew the feel of a solid base hit, the satisfaction of a difficult catch, and now he crosses into a new life and suddenly this woman is his. There never was any need to wonder, her world is his—

"You're crazy. Get out."

She is absolutely different. Sut looks at his plate. The food is all gone. Sut waits. He dreams. Things change. One day they are out, he and Ivy and the girl, only a baby from a picture over the fireplace. They walk through country fields to a picnic, the sun high and warm, a long day with nothing to hurry them, walking through woods, looking for the clearing. Everything moves slowly, birds sing deep notes, leaves on dark trees rustle with special meaning. Somewhere there is a clearing, a primitive campsite from long ago. They walk deeper into the woods, searching, surprised by bold shafts of light out of the green sky, pale green, sheltered in a deep wood, in a dark curtained room, thick air trapped behind dark woven drapes, forest patterned with hidden bright ruby and golden threads, living Birds of Paradise, the same bird again and again, red, green and grey philodendrons twine up the drapery, twining again, memories, woods and jungle scenes folded into forgotten byways, repeated like a chant, a woven chant, whole worlds circle around him he never knew, the room is stuffy, warmer, close, he slides, deeper, deeper like he is still in her belly, tiny and falling, gone, waiting, looking for morning and long night passes like a shadow, everything changes, when he emerges moist and wrinkled she is smiling, a new smile, *mater universa*, and he has come so far in no time:

"Stay for a while, Sut."

Well, how about that? Not an hour ago Sut was a ballplayer, a Washington Senator, one of the pros, up in the Bigs. He smiles. Stuck in seventh place. And now, in just one minute, he quit, of his own free will and not through any failure, no, he says, made my decisions and took my choices. Things are looking up. Anything may be ahead. He smiles at the bartender and another beer is on the way.

Light shines through green-and-gold windows. Just across the street and down the block is the nicest bar, a quiet neighborhood bar for Sut. Ivy will explain matters to the girl. Sapience is her name. All that Sut has seen of her is a photograph of her and Ivy over the mantel but that is old, taken years ago. The girl was only a baby and Ivy might have been anyone. He didn't look closely. The biggest room in the apartment belongs to Sapience, blocked off from the rest with a bed sheet.

Sut reaches for a newspaper and folds it open to the sports page. He reads about his friends. Another game today, starting—he looks at the clock—right about now.

If I hurried...I could tell Ralph I slept late. Not that he'd care. I might call up Bunyan after the game. Boy, he'd have something to say! 'Where the hell are you? What do you think you're doing?' Macy would say I was crazy to leave the team like that. And back home…Well, this might not even make the papers. I'll stay here, and then I'll go back, and tell her I quit.

Well. He looks at the floor. Who's to say I'm going back? She has cash money, plenty enough on hand, and with the brothers around there's always enough hands to run the farm. They don't expect me anyway until the season's over anyway. I've got enough cash myself to last that long, if need be. And then we'll see.

Another beer. He nods. It's not as if things were changing. I'll be back, I expect.

Drinking in the daytime—here comes the beer, yellow-gold, light airy foam, looks so much better in the daylight than at night, alive with sparkles and smiles. Another afternoon spent in a bar. Not for everyone, only millionaires and ballplayers can do that. A wonderful life, be a shame to leave it for something completely up in the air. Why did I leave? There's years yet, games to be played and one more time at the plate. The fans, that's really something. Folks all over the country know who you are, millions of them. They love the game, can't live without it and the game's always there, that's the thing, it never changes, all those people (the game, need only to hear, fleeting, late at night, a tired announcer with late final scores, games played a night ago or a year or ten, "Cleveland," he mumbles, and another city, static, lost details, "New York," again, crackles, interference, "fiveDetroittwo," the full meaning might escape you but the game, they did play, men dancing on the field in perfect order and it wouldn't matter, on the bench) waiting—

The hell it wouldn't. Just once more, one more goddam game, one time when I might. Sut tosses his cigaret. It hits the floor tip-first, hot red ember against black and white floor tiles, neat precise checks, worn spots where you might stand for hours and debate hopeless points end-lessly or watch the ballgame on TV—the cigaret lands and puts itself out. Perfect. He doesn't have to get up and snub the last bit out, rub it into the tiles like a thousand other drunks have done for—he looks around—thirty, fifty, too many years. No. The cigaret puts itself out, a superior toss by an old pro, yes indeed. Sut looks around the bar. Empty. What the hell.

Later he'll go home, reach for the key over the door, a new home, Ivy off to work and the girl—Sapience—working at her job too, he'll wait and this evening they will be at home together. A family where there was none. Something new beginning.

Sut sits on the couch. The apartment is so small, cut off from the city like a box, no reason for it, just a small partition. Cramped, nothing like the farm or a ballfield. If I stretch my arms out, it's almost wall to wall. Such a close life.

Nothing I'm doing will hurt anyone. We'll have a good time here and I'll stay or I'll leave, that's all there is to it. Not like it was a murder or anything. I'll go back to the farm later, tell her lies and feed her candy. Sut smiles. Years to come.

He puts his feet up and rests, full and accomplished, as he waits for things coming. A life in this tiny place might be fine and interesting. Tonight I'll meet her, we can talk. She isn't like that picture, I'm sure, that was taken years ago, only a baby then. Nothing to be done until then…

…watch the ceiling, lay back and stare at the plaster, lay back and think, wander, swirls among the cracks, old stories, only long-ago busy working men but so real, move with it, shapes and forms natural as any landscape, dream world, where he is, he wonders softly…a new life he's bargained for quick and easy as changing clothes, blundered into it by the slightest chance and here he is, moves with the plaster swirls and whips, gone from the team, his team, his life, wife, now Sut sits here in St. Louis and no idea of where to go, a whole new ball game, Sut and Ivy and Sapience, a way to look at things…

Sapience walks into the apartment hours later. Sut naps dreaming of bright patterned animals; he is sitting and they stroll past, smile at him and tell secrets he soon forgets. He looks up as Sapience hurries past, early-evening shadows hiding her, she slips between the curtains into her room sleek as an animal, gone without a ripple—he almost didn't see her. Not the larger baby-Sapience he had imagined, not a smaller Ivy, but her own self, short, compact, dark and sure.

She didn't see me. But Ivy told her I would be here. She knows. But not a word, nothing. Ivy's home later, she'll explain things again. We'll settle in together.

Dark night. Ivy opens the door hours later. Sut, on the couch, awake and asleep, sits up slowly—he doesn't know where he is. His shirt sticks, eyes are heavy, feet asleep and legs atingle, he's standing on sand, a mass of confused sensations—sees Ivy in the bright doorway, hard yellow light behind her, flat green vines on the wallpaper...

"Sut?" She moves across the room, a flick of her wrist and lights, lights, Sut flops back and rubs his eyes. "Why's it so dark in here, Sut? Where's Sapience? She's come home all right, hasn't she?" Ivy looks at him, a question, a small tremolo of fright in her voice. Sut pokes a thumb toward her room. Ivy hurries in. Sut shakes his head and adjusts his shirt. He stamps his feet. He can hear them talk, low murmurings, he can't make any words out but everything's fine, no worry, all is fine he is certain.

Ivy walks back out smiling, humming, takes off her light jacket and hangs it in a closet. "And neither of you could start anything for supper, hmm?" She turns, Sut watches, he knows her so well or not at all, she moves, a body under that dress, light grey and pink, designs in bells and bows, each side of the dress mirrors the other, pink on grey, grey on pink. He wants her. "You think you're at a free lunch counter, all you have to do is step up and take what you want?"

"Oh, no, I got money," Sut says, reaches for his pocket reflexively. He stops. That's not what she meant. "Didn't know when you were getting back," he says. "Uh, say, how's the girl? I didn't get a chance to meet her when she came in. I was out here dozing." He laughs. Ivy is in the kitchen, running water, the sounds of openings and closings, metal softly clashing, easy home sounds. She can't hear him. Sut gets up slowly, tests his weight on his tingling feet and walks into the kitchen.

"Would you call Sapience?" she says. "I'm going to be needing some help out here. And you can peel those potatoes over there." She hands him a paring knife. "Now."

He stands in the doorway looking at the knife. Nothing has changed. Last night, today, it seemed that Ivy was all his, things happening. Tonight she avoids his first clumsy embrace, accepts a light kiss. Now the world is so ordinary. He turns the knife in his hands, looks at it closely. So ordinary, like a knife. Ivy, at the stove, chatters brightly, random details from the day's work. A cheap short blade, ground to a point and chipped already, dull, rainbow-stained patina, bolted to a plastic handle. His knives, his wife's, were solid pieces, hollow-ground, bonded to the wood handle. Nothing. This knife. What could he possibly do with it?

"Would you call Sapience? Please?" Ivy looks at him. He stands in the doorway, turning the knife again and again in his big clumsy hands. He can use it after all. All that he has to do is peel the potatoes, sit at the table like any man and grab a potato, flick out the eyes, peel. The future could be new, hopeful, uncertain, the greatest or the smallest things might come from it. He and Ivy, Ivy as she is, unadorned, not a creature of his imagination and Sut no longer a ballplayer—

He could go back. He's missed just the one game and surely Bunyan covered for him some way. He could walk out the door and back to the hotel and be in the ballpark tomorrow afternoon. Ivy could sit in the stands and watch him again and the team would play and then pull up stakes, off on the road for the next series in—Chicago? Detroit?—and two months or so later the team would be back in St Louis again and Sut would walk right on over here.

Or he might go back tomorrow and Ralph would hand him the unconditional release.

"Never you mind. I'll go get her."

But anything might happen. The world is so wide, millions of corners and small details he will never know, places and facts, one false step among the ruins and he would plunge, fall aimlessly for years. But not if he stayed a ballplayer. This life need never end, just look at Petrarkis. The old and true patterns. The team, old and safe, they will always accept him, yesterdays today, swinging his golden flashing bat in an endless summer—Ivy will let him be a ballplayer forever. He couldn't go back even if he wanted.

Sut begins a new life. He smiles and laughs and quite easily steps over, the two of them will be together for this time although their points of contact are few.

"Tell me about that Jack Slade," she says. Her eyes are tired, shaded, as if thinking of a memory.

"Slade's going to do it," Sut says. "He's just about there, he's going to pull down that all-time record—"

"No, no, tell me about *Slade*." Ivy is a baseball fan too, but of stories, not numbers. "Did you ever know the man? What's he like?"

"He's good, he's good, if he gets the record he'll be the best ever."

"Oh, Sut, that's not true. Just because he has this record doesn't make him the best. And besides, there is Satchel Paige. Paige makes all those records meaningless."

"What? No, if he's got the most wins—"

"Nobody has won more games than Paige. Not a man, ever."

"This is the Bigs I'm talking about—"

"Sut! They wouldn't let him play! You know that!"

Well. That wasn't my fault.

She smiles. "There used to be other leagues, Sut. We had all-black leagues and we were as good or better than the majors. Where do you think all these fine young black players came from? Just sprang out of the ground? We had to play too, Sut. But they wouldn't let us into the majors. Where we belonged. We had a few—they called themselves 'Cubans,' somehow that was ok, Dolf Luque and others, jabbered like mock-Spanish and laughed behind your backs.

"We had our own leagues, and standings and champions, our own great stars. They called them the Negro National League, the Negro American. We had the St Louis Stars, Cool Papa played here, there were the Baltimore Elite Giants, New York Black Yankees, the Birmingham Barons, so many, Sut. Such fine young players, fine people and you'd never hear of any of them. And our leagues are all broken up now, the other leagues decided they wanted us, after all," she laughs, "and now they raid and take our best players away."

"Yeah, well, maybe, but that was still—it was different. Not the big leagues." A word is only a word to Sut. He grins, like a baseball card.

"Sut! Oh, Sut." She frowns. "You would have to be there, Sut. But it's all gone now. We played some games in Sportsman's Park, some in smaller parks, open fields or corner lots. Played the best of the white teams out barnstorming and we beat them. We put our best on the field, Sut, and Dizzy Dean, Bob Feller, Lou Boudreau, they all brought their best and damn it, we beat them."

"Aw—that was after the season, and all. The World Series was over, none of it counts until Opening Day again. That's like figuring spring training games."

"Sut. If you don't think those men were playing their best—"

"They couldn't have been. It wasn't during the season, they weren't under the gun."

"Oh!" She waves her hand, looks out the window. Off, gone back to an older world, watching the game that holds them together, another shape but the same game, the game. "Oh Sut, you'd have to be there to know, Satch Paige, Turkey Stearns, Josh Gibson. Josh Gibson…"

"Names, that's all."

"Oh, Sut! Just because they didn't keep track of the damn numbers so well, just because it was so much looser, fluid and open, Sut, we still had the game. The same rules, the same ball. Maybe the players jumped from team to team on their own, 'stead of letting the owners jump them around, maybe we didn't play in the best ballparks and the ideal conditions and the right number of umpires and new balls whenever you snap your fingers but, Sut, oh Sut…

"Maybe it wasn't teams we had but we had the players, the best, we had our stories too, not any stats. No numbers, Sut. Why should there have to be numbers?

"There was Josh Gibson, Sut. He was better than Babe Ruth. One year he hit this many home runs, so many more than Ruth, and more, more than that in another year. More than Babe Ruth. And he hit the ball farther than Babe Ruth."

Sut smiles. Yeah, sure.

"Laugh if you want, Sut. But he was better. If he hit some of those homers in small ballparks and off semi-pro pitchers, well, that wasn't his fault. If he hit some in wide-open fields or under shabby lighting or with balls all cut up and scuffled that you could *never* hit square, that wasn't his fault either. Josh could hit the ball as hard, as far, harder, further, wouldn't matter if it was you or me or Dizzy Dean on the mound.

"They say he died of a brain tumor but that wasn't it. One day, in January in the very same year Jackie Robinson took the big leagues, Josh, he had retired only a few years before, he went up to bed and asked his brother to go out and pick up all his trophies. They were scattered all over town, he had given them out to all his friends over the years. So his brother gathered up all the trophies, all the friends, and Josh's radio too. His brother got them all together and they were talking and Josh just died.

"And it wasn't any brain tumor he died of, Sut. Suppose *you* were better than Babe Ruth but they wouldn't let you prove it?"

"Why'd you quit that team, Sut? Wasn't all for me, was it?"

He looks at her. Cigaret smoke drifts by, she taps her fingers, nails painted bright red, her face thin and hard. If he looks closely there are tired bloodshot veins, fading flesh and daily worries. They've lived together for days. Sut's team has left town.

"Was it, Sut?"

Of course it was, of course not. She's glad he quit, Sut knows that much, glad that she could lure him from the game, the team and the society of men, and that feeds her. Sut should say yes, yes, everything for you like a movie with Ronald Colman, sweep her away and—

"Because I knew we were going to lose." He stops, keeps his distance. There are worlds he won't cross over, too many dragons, too many trials. Ivy sits up. Sut frowns. "It finally got to me. Every game—not *every* game, but always that feeling, any time the game would just fall apart, that we were going to lose again and again."

"Worried about losing?" So ridiculous, like a boy with a stolen lie, words out of nowhere sadly, but words, she must contend with words. "Oh, Sut. You didn't know you were losing before? Playing there on the worst team in baseball and can't even break into the starting lineup and you didn't know—"

He looks at her. You know what I mean. Don't you? "Oh hell, I knew that, I guess," he says. "I knew we would never win the pennant, damn it, or we wouldn't beat the Yanks or win a big game against Cleveland or Slade, this game or that one. But all we ever did, game after game, was lose. And all they count in our league is the wins."

"So you think you'd just quit?"

"I did, didn't I?" he snaps. "You can't win, and I'll be damned if there's any way you can, you just go out there, and every game you just get older until finally you're gone." Sut rubs at a stain on the table cloth, not cloth but a rubberized plastic, pushes his stubby fingers across the pattern and wishes he could say things, why he quit, older stories, if it

was winning and losing it still had nothing to do with sport, nothing he
knows any words for.

Some day, he knows, he will forget every game he has played, put his
hand to the plow and never think to look back. But today he is in this
kitchen, staring at a strange woman he doesn't know the least of, waiting…He licks his finger and rubs at the small purple stain roughly but it
won't come out, Ivy talks and he thinks of what he might have said,
something else.

Sut looks at Ivy. Now she is silent. Long minutes they don't move. In
the other room there is a photograph, on the mantel above the cold fireplace. Ivy is dressed in a uniform or a dress much like a uniform, holding baby Sapience on her lap, the photo in brown sepia tones and a big
gold deco border. Sut imagines how she was then. Quickly, before the
war began. She doesn't speak, there is a question on her face, Sut is tired
of questions, no more questions.

"What…" she says.

They were playing, he remembers. Little Sut, then, sitting behind a
fencepost, dabbling in the bright mud, black mud, new spring drown-
ing in wonderful odors, no invisible lines between his dreams and the
daytime, anything in his mind is possible in the mud, he laughs—

Far across the field he sees boys in the open pasture, playing. He
watches, fascinated, moves closer, watches—how they move! Patterns
where he never would have expected, an order and a calling and now he
runs, chases the ball, all lost in games. He grabs the ball and throws it,
up, high in the sky, laughs and watches, the ball falls—

Later they show him the game, hand down the rules like rituals. Sut
can still remember his first hit and scoring, touching all the bases.
Time passes and he plays games as if that were all there were, throwing
a tennis ball against the barn for hours, thinking himself Dizzy Dean
putting away the best that Greenberg and the Tigers had to offer, bat-

ter after batter. Every bounce off the wall had a meaning, hit, walk, out, cowpie errors.

In high school, only a sophomore, he is the best player in the county. Every time he makes the right move, never thinking. When he pitches, he gets by on main strength. At sixteen they offer him a pro contract and laughing, running, he drops out of school and goes off to Appleton, Lancaster, up the ladder to Savannah. Every winter he comes back to the farm and one year he takes a wife and borrows to buy his own farm. Some day, he thinks during every game he plays, I will make the Big Show. But he does. He hangs on for five years, plays with the men he knew in the minors, years before, counterpunching, reacting and guessing right along with the rest of them. There always was a lot more bad players than good, Bunyan said once, hardly smiling.

Late at night when the lights are out and nothing to see he thinks back over seasons past, the game, the years, playing along by the rules. The rules. They will get me by. Just follow right along. Swing the bat. Run to first, then second, third and home. Hell, I'm the guy they put dotted lines on the boxes for: Open here. Just go along with the game (but it was never that simple and even Sut knows it. Macy showed him the spirit of adaptation and imagination, Inside Baseball, Bunyan understood the game instinctively, Ralph lived it, Ivy with her shadow leagues, Slade living in deeper dark regions of the game, every place where the rules are only a starting-point and a hint of what might be done) and play.

Now when he sleeps in her arms pictures come to his mind, not words, no rules, but colors from where life might have lead, movement without rules, running into deep green purpling sunsets past slim poplars twisting, laughing with fairy-tale voices, long dusty afternoons, frosty-patterned nights, iron crystal winters, and springtime meant more—when he returns, young again—more than games, green pushing out of the dirt everywhere, again and again, signs, life on the land never ends and he knows, for once he knows, no questions, where he

will land. The game—however he tries, whatever he does, he is innocent, without guile, lost in a forest.

They play games. Sut competes, still looks for winners and losers,
nothing can change that so quickly. One night they drink beer together,
sitting at the kitchen table and listening to Ivy's radio. Sut is domestic,
settled, happy and unaware of the outside world. The radio cries,
strange music. She won't let him tune in his stations even though he is
sure there is good country music in St Louis. Her songs are pulsing,
with an insistent demanding beat, too anxious for him, soaring ago-
nized guitars, voices like dying.

"Can't find anything better than that? Here, let me—"

"Sut." She pulls at her cigaret quickly, flares the smoke out her nos-
trils, puts a hand on the radio. "Things are just fine. Now settle down.
I've got to slow myself, can't keep matching you drink for drink." She
smiles at him. "Got to get my sleep. Tomorrow, maybe the day after too,
I have to work some on overtime. Got to buy sis a new coat. They're on
sale right now and she wants to look good this fall. I can't blame her.
Back to school and all those boys just chasing after her—"

"She ought to be home, not staying with friends all the time." Ivy
keeps them apart, a distance Sut doesn't understand. He wants a family.
In the father's place, he makes and preserves the generations. Sut understands, or thinks he does. He turns around and the gaps are so wide, so
many disappointments in their young life together.

"And why should you have to work extra tomorrow? I've got money.
We should go out tomorrow anyway." Randolph Scott is in town. Sut
wants to run in the streets until late. But if she works she has to be in
early. Can't fall asleep while bending stacking and sorting, she tells him.
"Or you could just go down to the Salvation Army," he says. "They've
got all that stuff."

Sut looks at his beer can: A brown mountain range, Schlitz! on a belt buckle 'round a globe, a huge promise, a world of merry beer drinkers. He crushes the can in his hand and sights the wastebasket.

"That's what they have those places for," he says.

"Folks like us?" she asks brightly. How weary, stale, flat and unprofitable seem all the uses of this world. Nothing changes. He flips the can, a high graceful arc, soon as I let it go I knew it was good, he would have told long chorus—Ivy smiles and moves like a snake, flicks the can away.

"We were looking through the winter catalogs before—a while ago, and now the sales are on, she has the one she wants all picked out. So I'm working, Sut. It's not always so easy."

"Well, if you have to buy a new one. You'd be surprised what you can come up with, though. These old moneybags wear them once, spill a cocktail or their cats sleep on 'em, then they just toss them out the window."

"Sut."

"Well." He pauses and looks around the small kitchen. There are no more surprises for him. He knows the clock above the stove is always five minutes fast, that there are delicious chocolate-chip cookies in that jar on the counter. A back doorway leads out, down twisting stairs to the noisy street below. Everything up here is crowded, hot, sticky.

"That's not what I mean. You know..." She does, she must. Sut drums the table. The room is too small, when he moves anywhere in the apartment everything is too close, he could stumble over something and break it or smash the whole apartment. The garbage can in the corner is full, the garbage has soured and must be taken out. Sut could do that. The beer can is on the floor nearby.

"Sut." She waits. The walls are yellowed, old ancient grease stains forever above the stove, too many years of apartment lives and passing faces. Ivy scrubs but no use. Time passes and age shows.

She never talks about the future. She knows what is coming, puts everyday happenings into words that last forever. Sut wants to ask her, but he has not the first idea and although she would never tell him, she would ask, and he'd say Success, I guess. But you had that, she'd say, and you can't go back, so what are you doing here? And he would say, Yes, but I never thought of it that way.

Sut walks through the apartment. Ivy is working, Sapience is out with her friends. By now he should know their comings and goings but he has no idea, they might be back at any moment or not for hours. He wonders about her life, small things she would never think to tell him. Maybe something she owns, a personal detail stamped out on an assembly line or woven on a huge mechanical loom.

Ivy's apartment is the top floor of a duplex, brick and very square. The rooms are small, close and intense. On his farm the house is immense, room after room, more than he and his childless wife could ever possibly use, every room sunlit and clean-white painted. In winter when he is home the rooms are cold, empty and echoing. They stay mostly in the warm kitchen and parlor, a central space, not much larger than Ivy's apartment.

He stands in the kitchen and looks into the back bedroom. She keeps almost nothing, no personal memories. In the morning the kitchen is square and bright yellow, squirrels run along the back porch railing, wrens sing in the trees. He turns. The bedroom is to his right and the hallway leads to the main room, the television room, what he would call a parlor back in Iowa. Beyond this is a larger room partitioned off with a flowered sheet: Sapience's room. He has never been in there.

He turns again and walks back through the apartment, so quickly. Each room has a new scent, its own flavor, not like his scrubbed-clean white farmhouse. The first aroma here, as he opened the door, on the very first night was strong pleasant musk, warm and soft, his new world. The kitchen always smelled like toast.

He belongs here, he says, in this apartment, in Ivy's St. Louis time. Hide away, the old life is past. He doesn't feel any guilt. He waits. Will he go back? Sut pokes around the apartment, sifts through magazines. He studies the porcelain and glass flower arrangements on the empty bookshelves. Christiana is fine, he knows. His wife back home (the phrase never leaves him) is well attended, his brothers are neighbors and she has her garden. Sut himself is in a new life, gone. A new world. He can do it, bridge the gap, live out all the promises and—

On a shelf high above the fireplace he finds a small collection of baseball cards. They aren't hidden, but put away carefully. Sut climbs a chair to fetch them down. There are two stacks, one much smaller than the other, and tied together with thick red rubber bands. He sorts through them like a schoolboy.

The smaller pile has several of Slade's cards. One of them, a drawing rather than a photograph, is from back in his Cardinal days. Sut's rookie card, his very first, is in the pile. Wide moon-faced farmer-ballplayer, happy empty smile, little gaps in the teeth and a cartoon ballplayer drawn in the lower corner: 'Sut McCaslin, Outfield, Washington Nationals.' Everything, anything, back then when anything was possible.

He flips the card away. Bunyan, Ramose, some Brownies and Cardinals, other players through the leagues. Except for Slade, none of the big ones. No Yankees, no stars. A funny collection, players you really didn't think of when you thought about the game. And a picture of the Kid Ebony, not a baseball card but a newspaper photograph, glued to cardboard and carefully cut to the right shape. Sut turns it over. No stats. The Kid is a rookie, in baseball, and doesn't have his first real card yet. Small ink markings in all the margins, stars, crosses, mystery shapes. He sets the pile down.

Wait—that top one. Sut picks it up and looks closely. A picture of Slade, but not one of his baseball cards. Slade in a suit. A real photograph, one you'd take with your own camera, in here with the baseball cards. Sut looks at it again, closely, then wraps them all up again in the rubber band.

The other group has Ned Garver, Jim Delsing, Bobby Avila, Bob Friend. The movie stars. Most of the Yankees are here too. Bauer with a face like a fist. Billy Martin looking mean as Armando's stiletto, Berra the gnome and Mantle from out of the clouds. Other stars, Kaline, Minoso, more. Why two piles, Sut wonders. Best to leave 'em right. He puts them back just as he found them.

He looks around the apartment again. He doesn't know what he was looking for but he didn't find it. There is Sapience's room, behind the curtain. He stops. Only a flowered print, a faded field of posies on a sheet, not even a door. He can walk right in if he wants. Sapience is gone, he is alone in this apartment. Sut parts the fold, opens the curtain, he shouldn't, he doesn't go in. He stares at himself. He moves, blunders, smiles...

Directly across the room there is a mirror, a vanity. He sees himself reflected in this room, in this apartment, as far as ever from anything he knows, holding onto a sheet. Who is Sapience, Sut wonders. He steps back out of her room.

He never sees Sapience. When she is home, Ivy keeps them apart in this tiny apartment. He doesn't know why, or if there is a reason or a mystery. Sometimes a hanging sheet is enough. He lets it fall.

He wonders about Sapience's father. What could he have been? 'Pretty as an Indian,' Ivy said one night about the girl. Or was he a King Bechuana? Sut imagines dark mysteries, men in steamy jungles wrestling huge lions. But Ivy never mentions anyone. There's nothing he's seen in here that tells him anything. The only photographs inside the apartment besides the baseball cards are the ones hanging over the mantel, Ivy and Sapience, some older men and women, family. He supposes but he never knows.

Once Ivy left the two of them alone together in the parlor. Sut looked at her. She looked out the window. He thought how strange it was, all he knew about Ivy, the woman in her passion that Sapience would never know, but balanced against all the girl's thousand details and half-memories, stories Sut would never hear, could never understand. She sat without moving, cool dark skin, motionless with her stories. Sut couldn't look at her. Suppose Ivy came back in. Or if she looked back.

Sut looks out the window. Nothing moving on the street. He walks through the apartment again. Who is Sapience, Sut wonders.

He settles in the parlor like any bored ballplayer, silently watching the air. The world strolls by, ignoring him casually. Things work out, he says, they always will. Nothing will rock old Sut.

Here I sit, he thinks.

Sut hasn't been to a ballpark since he pinch-hit against the Browns and that was—how long ago? He looks out the window. The Senators are still losing. Sut left and nothing changed. He had thought about going to see the team when they played their final game in St. Louis. He could have worn dark glasses, maybe a false beard, and sat in the bleachers. Asked for autographs after the game. But he hadn't gone.

Sut wanted badly to talk to Bunyan. Nothing important, just ask about the team, the latest stories, what Macy was up to, was Ralph dozing off on the bench. About playing the game. He could have called up the hotel when the team was in town or he could send a letter to the ballpark. But he doesn't like to write and he knows the first thing Bunyan will say is 'Where the hell are you and what the hell do you think you're doing?' And Sut will be damned if he knows.

Every Sunday he reads the sports pages carefully. He runs his fingers down the lists of batting averages and identifies his old friends. Bunyan—this year he's right up there, Sut sees. John is in the hunt. Batting a solid three-fortyfive, his best ever, way ahead of the team, hitting at a champion's pace in any league—except this year, except this league. Mantle and Williams and someone, Bunyan is right behind someone, not this year for Bunyan.

And there is the greatest sports headline—'Slade in Bid for Record.' The pages are crowded with numbers, comparisons, old facts brought swiftly to light, Young's achievements from fifty years past and Slade's from last summer, wins, losses, height and weight. Slade, moving through time, is living history, *pteraspis*, Slade the walking fossil, a man passed out of baseball generations. He tied the ancient record, Slade ascendant, in a shaky game against the A's, a sloppy thirteen to nine win.

These days Slade suffers from invisible wounds, stigmata that not everyone could see. Over the course of the season he has discovered the human limits to the game, absolute and predestined numbers, final statistics for any man. He starts only a single game each week, pitches infrequently in short relief. He is haggard, stone features chiseled hollow, the coldest light in his eye. Another man would have retired years ago, handed in his walking papers and accepted what congratulations there were, but Slade will pitch, will win, will find that final win.

Today, Slade says.

The Tigers end the season on the road, St. Louis, Chicago, wandering in the West. Slade won't set his records in front of hometown fans. Other mileposts set up by long chorus—three hundred wins, four hundred, passing Walter Johnson, thirty wins in a season—were all set on the road.

Hometown, Slade snorts. Between the lines, he says. Foul line to foul line. All the home I will need.

"Ivy!" Sut calls. "Ivy! Let's go to the ball game today." She walks in from the kitchen. "Don't you want to get out to the ballpark, catch a game? The season's just about gone. This is damn near last chance."

Ivy watches him. Not every day does she go to work. She's been to a few games when Sut wouldn't go out. She didn't say. She wanted to see the Kid play. She won't say anything now. If Sut decides they will go to a ballgame, then they will go.

"And a damn big game, too. Slade is going to set that record right here in St. Louis." He holds up the sports page.

"Can you get tickets?"

Today's game is big. Not in the standings; the teams are settled firmly into fifth and seventh. This game has meaning beyond the bounds of quotidian statistics, streaks and pennant races. Slade is rewriting the history books as he pitches himself to baseball immortality. Thousands of fans will be at the game and tens of thousands more will claim they had been. Tickets are scarce but lucky Sut is no ordinary fan. He has connections.

"I can call up Tindall on the Tigers. He was on the Senators for a couple years, we went out drinking a lot. He'll get us tickets." Won't say anything about running into me either. He might not even know I've been gone.

"Hey, and there's this other player—the Ebony. I only saw him play the one time but he had all the makings. I see by the papers he's doing damn good. A real ballplayer."

Today's game is one for all time, history on the hoof, a celebration of America.

Every ceremony, every ritual will be brought to bear on the game. Today it is Slade against the Kid, baseball memories of Grover Alexander pitching to Ruth, Christy Mathewson versus Honus Wagner, Feller dueling DiMaggio. Sut is ready for the game. He smiles.

"Let's stop in over there. We can't walk all the way out to Sportsman's without a drink. Looks like a nice bar too, a quiet one."

Sut points across the street to a low solid building, Midwest modern, red brick facade and small curtained windows, a trace of neon, a quiet bar in a friendly neighborhood. The front door is open in the noontime heat, soft country music sings to the street, soft laughter floats out, the sound of tinkling glass.

"One thing about St. Louis," Sut strides across the street and in the door, "you never have to look too far to find a bar."

Ivy follows him in. The room is dark in the daytime, unlit but for the light from the doorway. Men pause and laugh from far corners of the bar, a cigaret flare illuminates a face, a quick gargoyle, rough laughter, tragedy and comedy.

"And baseball fans too. Look." Sut points to the wall. Autographed pictures of hometown players, Musial, Slade ('Best Wishes,' writes Musial while Slade signs only his name, an angry scar), Enos Slaughter and Ned Garver lined up behind the bar, team photographs across the room. At the far end of the bar are two uniforms, Cardinals' home whites with a cheery redbird perched on a bright yellow bat and next to it a grey Brownie road suit, hanging on pegs and ready for any game.

"That's what I like to see," Sut says. "Maybe I ought to tell the folks who I am."

"Was," Ivy says.

Sut turns around on his stool and leans against the bar. He squints into the gloom at the tables. Most seem to be empty, a few couples and small groups here and there. In this town, in this bar, I would be an enemy ballplayer. A foreigner. They'd boo and hiss in the ballpark but they'd be glad to know me here, even an enemy can tell stories out of the dugout and locker room, what it's like to be out on the diamond. He smiles, huge and vacant. They would be as excited with a major league player as he is with his fans.

Ivy drinks. She hunches over the bar, ought not to be here, not to be out drinking, not out with this big dumb old ballplayer, going to a ballgame, not…How does life go? It wouldn't be right to laugh just now. She watches the bartender closely, he so deft with the bottles, no shot glass, pouring drinks both generous and charming. She smiles. He frowns.

There is nothing to be afraid of, live in this world the way you see it, live, satisfied mind. Is that right or wrong?

Who are these people? Who are ballplayers? Little kids, always little, lost and appealing, make you want to be families and raise them up but who belongs where? She laughs, silently.

Sut turns around smiling. "Nice place," he says. He points to her drink and waves at the bartender. "Yes, yes."

She can see Sut in the mirror, watch him looking without looking at him, watch the people watching him. What they think, what they know about themselves. She should explain for him, everything at once, tell him in a word where they are and what will happen, now and the future, what lies ahead. But she won't, she waits.

"You know, buddy. Hey, listen here. You know who you are, after all." The man is small but he has a big mouth. Sut turns to look at him. Big red lips, red-checked shirt flaring out of his pants, black eyes, short and mean.

Sut doesn't know—why is the man there? A black moment of doubt comes toward him like a fist, he stumbles, the man dances. "Coming in here, you know. With that—" Sut moves. He doesn't think. The man struts, waves his arms stiffly, jabbers and lunges. Sut slips and the little man-animal is all over him, pounds, swarms, balls his tiny fists and pounds, tiny stings all over Sut, he roars, pants, he backs off and bumps the stool, bounces off the bar, Brute pounds on his back, pulls Sut forward, rants senseless curses, jumps on his back, Sut is so confused, he doesn't feel a thing, doesn't know, all he sees is Brute's face grow and expand like a balloon, a flesh-and-bloodling balloon suddenly released and atop Sut, he only reacts, pulled under, stings, stings, he thinks starkly in black and white: Lift him, grab the legs and lift him, Sut imagines a statue like Antaeus, he wants to end it, erase and forget like nothing happened—

Before Sut can grab and lift Brute, pull the switch, the fight is suddenly over. All the hands are on them, grab them and pull them apart, "C'mon now, quiet it down," men pull them apart, Sut does not resist, "Hey man you in public, act right," the little man still jerks and twists, bugged eyes staring at Sut.

Sut sits. The fight is over as soon as it began. They pull the little man away, push him out the back door while he screams blood curses and violence, now out the door and gone. Sut looks at the floor. His mind is empty. He wants only to reverse time, such a cheap trick, erase the last five minutes as if they had never happened. His shirt has a small tear. No one in the bar looks at him. Maybe they all forgot and it never did happen. No one knows him. He'll slip out the door and everything will be over and forgotten. He hurries to the door.

Where's Ivy? Sut looks around quickly, standing in the doorway. Nowhere. Good. Maybe she didn't see the fight. He walks into the street. But she must have. She was there when it started. Damn, I looked pretty bad. But I could have whipped him, if I had a little more time. But I couldn't raise a scene. I'll have to explain to her.

There she is, down the street. He thinks to call after he then sees she is headed toward the ballpark. He follows, slowly.

Entire families, roving packs of males, individual fans swarm in the stadium streets awaiting the game. There is a buzz in the ballpark, excitement rarely tasted this late in the season. Ancient ballplayers have returned from the far shores of retirement on pilgrimage for this game. Even the aged Young is in attendance, surrounded by red-white-and-blue bunting, sitting in a special box. Long chorus relishes the ceremony and imagines writing a message for all eternity.

The Browns take the field to begin the game. Slow and tired men go through their motions, springtime is gone, summer gone, the game in autumn. The Kid moves through them like mercury.

"Sut," Ivy says as she stares at the Kid.

"You'd think you'd never seen one of those before, the way you're eyeballing him," says Sut. He slumps in his seat as he would on the bench. He wants to leap over the railing, tear away his street clothes to reveal a baseball uniform and play the game again.

"Oh Sut." Ivy watches the Kid, liquid motion on the diamond. "Sut, he is *so* pretty."

Pretty. Sut laughs. What does that mean? Sut's seen pictures of the Kid, watched him across the field. He's just a man, with that huge forehead and tiny eyes, pinholes of fire, so intense, a true ballplayer. "Ugly sunuvabitch," Sut says. "Hell of a ballplayer, though."

"And pretty. So pretty. The way he moves, look at the way he moves out there. Just so damn pretty."

Sut looks at Ivy. He forgets he knows her. Only her eyes...Her face opens up and years dissolve; on the field the Kid, twisting and diving, plucks the ball out of the air. So pretty.

Sut moves him in different directions. There is a glow to the Kid, something seen so briefly elsewhere before, so rare, an aura, a monster drive in the man that won't be denied. But damn if he is pretty.

Slade no longer warms up. He is never on the field before the game. He stands alone somewhere in the huge concrete ballpark, away from all eyes, in a private space. Then he turns and walks quickly, with a slight jerking limp, out to the field, paces up the dugout and sits and the umpire calls Play ball.

Once underway the game today moves, the game plays like any other. Detroit scores two easy runs in the top of the first and the Kid homers leading off for St Louis and the score stays at two to one for innings.

Slade pitches rapidly, wastes nothing, a master at his craft. The malaise of summer is gone. He has recovered all of baseball's gifts. One bad pitch to the Kid and now he runs the game, an old-time rheumy-eyed billiards player, figures the angles and breaks like a dream in his mind, paces and breaks pace, racks up the Brownies again and again.

In the fourth he steps out of his game to hit the Kid with a primitive fastball. The Kid rises and they look across the diamond at one another.

Later in the game the Brownies' pitchers collapse, Detroit scores nine runs over the last three innings, the game is over, Slade has won. Slade is first. Young is second. Slade has stopped time.

Slade can leave the game whenever he wants, silently accept the last booming wave of applause from the stands then disappear from their sight forever. He talks to Gardiner in the dugout and says he will finish the game. One last game.

The Kid bats in the ninth. The game is over. Slade pitches and the ball grazes the Kid's cap. The umpire shakes his head, points to Slade in slight admonishment. Slade rocks into his motion.

The Kid doesn't move. He must see it—you call to him. The ballpark is silent. Slade darts like a viper and the ball shoots, a fascinating rocket smack! flush against the Kid's forehead and straight up, the ball floats twenty feet into the air, the Kid drops.

House jumps. He looks down the bench. "Abelmann. Get in there and run for him." Abelmann doesn't think. The old man calls time and runs to first base. House walks to the plate. The Kid doesn't get up.

"Goddam you, listen! Christ, a hundred damn years ago I could have bought you—" His voice is loud, too loud. The words fade, the room is still, empty as ice. He wants to speak, wants to say something. His arms hang, huge hands open and close on nothing. He looks up.

"Yes you could have." Did she say that? Or the television…Sut reaches. He would relax and joke, he would. No argument, no fight. Smile and laugh. But he can't relax, he is too stiff and tired. He can't look at her. He stares straight ahead.

The TV plays in the corner.

"The goddam TV."

The senator is with them, he babbles, hard TV lights reflect off him as he snickers then points a raging finger.

"The goddam TV! Why do you leave the sunuvabitch on!" Sut runs over to the set, slaps it, runs his hand across to the knob and snaps it off. She looks at him. She seems bored, her eyes are empty.

In his mind's eye they might be posing for a photograph, it's that formal. Sut stands behind her as she sits, his hands on her shoulders and she holds tightly to one thick hand. They stare straight ahead. Neither moves.

"Sut," she says. "Sut. What do you think of."

He doesn't know. He wants to stand there, not moving, forever. She tightens her hand on his.

"Sut. You aren't playing a game are you."

He doesn't say a word. He looks down to her. She twists round, looks up to him even and steady.

He looks at her. His mouth works slowly, gasping, a landed fish.

Ivy has gone to work on the night shift. He walks out the door and thinks of an old hymn he used to sing in church, years ago, 'strait is the gate,' discipline, rigor, 'and narrow the way.' His wife is at home. She is bothersome, he thinks, fussy, tender. She will always be there. They never fight, she will never wonder, they reflect each of them the other.

The television in the corner is on. Leave it. The Hearings are playing. To hell with it, he says.

He closes the door, worlds away. He should hurry down to the depot and see when the buses leave. He can decide which one he wants when he gets there. He will not take a thing with him. The extra clothes he bought might fit the next ballplayer. He had thought about bringing them. He could leave a note and scatter the clothes throughout the city, made her look for them piece by piece. But he departs without a thing from this world, leaves it as he came.

He leaves, he scatters and disperses, more and more things are Sut, always a something, a shape, a form he won't ever go beyond, he might stick his head into black nothing void and gawk in awe at emptiness, but things, says Sut, are good and bad, black and white although everything in life shows him just the opposite: One spring day, thousands of tiny shoots newly popped from the ground, deep blue sky rolling back forever, empty brown road winding and flowing across distant hazy hills, over the landscape, nearby stream gurgling, woods chirping full of life...He shuts off his tractor and stands on the seat, silent as a statue, shields his eyes and waits. A single deer stands motionless against the trees, a flick and gone: nothing is opposite, all opposites are lies, Sut sees this but never says, never knows and now—

He's gone and he thinks he should sum up, for himself, days out of his memory, time, days, weeks, a season. In his mind he thinks he will balance all that's happened. He sees Ivy, across the two worlds, she stands solidly on her globe and smiles at him as they fly violently apart into deep endless space, among immense beings, lordly masks without faces, impassive unending movement. Sut can't get anywhere. The image of masks is enough for him. He wins small human success and keeps himself quietly.

Far down the street he can see the depot. It shouldn't be this close but there it is, ablaze in the night, all white, plastic alabaster, a Babylonian temple floating above the street. The street is long, very long. The depot may be farther away than it seems. It is late at night and the stores are all closed but light and colors are everywhere, windows on fire with the coldest light—Sut knew this color once before, in a dream, the glowing forever flourescent light of a structure that-would-never-move...He passes through the lights, other colors, night neon dark lights dance over him, his skin now green and blue, dark pulsing orange, red throbbing red; he sheds one color easily as another. People on the street stand forever in the bright islands under street lamps, sleek nighthawks dart and vanish and then rematerialize in a further streetlight or closer or never again. Up stairs are downtown apartments, quick lights, more lives and stories Sut will never know. So many...

He stops. Things may change yet: The air clears, he breathes deeply, everything is wide and true, he can make the jump and just now the sky parts, real light pours out but he can't move, he only waits and the moment passes, dips out of sight and Sut walks on down the street.

Down the street he sees her: Ivy. She is spotlighted in the night under a streetlight, wearing a dress all crimson and flowing; silken and liquid night creatures swim in the edges of the light, now stirring with frantic rhythm, a dark bladeswift man in the shadows, in the light, moving with cool selfknowledge, sharp applegreen suit and blinding snakeskin loafers, he looks up and laughs and Sut recognizes the Kid, the dead gone Kid back again, that dark intense man, was he one man or two, Sut stands and stares and they glide near to him, Sut can't move, the heat subsides, Ivy stands on the edge of a pool of light and touches his arm. So far apart. Ivy and Sut stand in the light, the light moves.

He looks into her eyes but he sees only perfect reflection, only himself looking back and then a pebble drops and ripples run through her eyes, the night comes rushing back, she moves silkily to the Kid, they melt, the night is empty again and Sut stands alone under the streetlight, night fades, the day eases in, slow greys, purples, dead pinks and the lamps blink out, Sut stands in the naked day, falls in step with the accelerating traffic.

The depot is only a short block away.

HOME

◆

Yankee Stadium—big! There had never been such a ballpark before! The cab turns a corner and abruptly, suddenly, all you can see, there it stands! A Colosseum on pillars of American Gothic, the House that Ruth Built: Sut imagines the hero with one mighty swing of his bat as he creates the edifice. The cabdriver turns partway round and smiles. Yessir, he points, there it is, would you take a look at those pennants!, Sut nods at the rows of silk flags fluttering from the rafters, thousands of games won, World Championships, the greatest team ever in the history of the game. The cabdriver looks at his meter and Sut gets out. He scoops in his pocket for change and fills the man's hands. He walks through the players' gate and into the ballpark. No one stops him, no questions asked. Stadium attendants wave, sure, that's ol' Sut, they say, go on in. Do they know he's been gone? He stands in the clubhouse door. Bunyan smiles. What could Sut say? He walks over to his locker. His uniform hangs neatly on a peg, spikes polished and shiny. Across the room Macy is in a noisy argument. The door to Ralph's office is open and Sut can see Ralph and Keyser huddled over a lineup card. Sut changes into his uniform.

"Last game today," says Bunyan. "They're sure to get you in the game somewhere."

"Yeah," Sut smiles. "Didn't want to come all this way just to sit on the bench."

"Hey," Macy calls and walks over to them, clumsy in shower sandals, wearing only a baseball cap and a towel wrapped around his middle, "these guys are trying to tell me the season's over. Don't want to play today. Christ, can you imagine that?

"It's these rookies come up looking for the big chance and then they get cold feet. We was never that way. We knew what we had to prove. They just don't know how it's anything can happen, see, even the last day of the year. There's games, there's pennants to be won." Macy pokes his face, a mask of disgust, into every corner of the locker room.

"John, you've got to tell them how you won that run-batted-in crown. You remember, back in '50, '51. Beat out Zernial on the last day of the season. We was playing the A's, you remember, Zernial's team, you and him head to head on the same diamond and you took him, John," says Macy, who's never won more than a paycheck. "That's how the great ones are gonna do it, out on the field under the gun, all the pressure, see, that's the—"

"Nobody's winning anything today, Seth." Bunyan bounces a ball on the concrete floor. "Everything's been decided, nothing more to be said about this season. It's the Yankees once again, and the fair-haired Mantle's won everything under the sun." John looks at Sut and smiles.

"Sometimes you have a little hope. Gave it a try this year, got a hot streak and started to see my name in the headlines, pushed some, but damn I should have known better. Couldn't bring it off. Getting too old now. You know, Seth, that RBI title is the only thing I've ever won. No batting titles or nothing."

"Just two, three points shy that one year."

"Short is short." They thought about baseball but talked like old men. "There's a limit, you know." John looks at them. Even his teammates expect him to be a hero. He tries, he does his job, isn't that enough? "Well, you aren't born with it," he says. "They don't give it to you either.

Christ, so what else is new? You'll have me taking this shit seriously, Seth. It's a game. Throw the ball and hit it. That's all."

"John, you haven't come all this far if it's only a game. There's one hell of a lot more there and you know it. You know what all these people..." Macy waves vaguely. He shrugs and paddles back to his locker, calls to the vets and glares at the young players. Game's a game, this is the Game.

"Where's Hardy?" asks Sut. So many new faces in the locker room, the September rookies.

"Hardy? They released him—too old." John smiles, pulls on his cap. "But there's a game today. Hurry, Sut." John leaves.

Sut pulls on his cleats and ties them carefully. He looks in the little mirror in his locker and adjusts his cap, square on his head. Just right. The room is now empty and quiet, only soft echoes of the game, almost deserted. Macy, dressed for the game now, sits in front of his locker.

"Hey." He waves to Sut. "Come on over here. Something happened." Seth sits alone, two pebbles in his hand, clack clack. "The damnedest thing, you wouldn't believe it. I didn't tell anyone because I didn't think they would a believed it, but it happened, Sut. The Yankees made an offer for me. Can you imagine? They wanted to pick up a spot infielder who knew the league, someone who'd been around. Just to finish the season, see, then they'd release me. Insurance for the breaks, see."

He plucks at his drab uniform. "Me—in pinstripes." He pulls at his cap, down tight over his skull. "See, Martin's in the Army now. Coleman's good but he's getting old. Like me. They offered two pitchers from the low minors and some cash. Owner was interested but he turned them down. He wanted a thousand bucks, or maybe only a few hundred, more.

"I would a paid the money myself, Sut. I got cash saved. But he turned them down and the Yankees went someplace else. I never knew until later.

"Hey," says Macy as they walk out to the diamond. "The Yankees is a sure thing."

Sut sits on the bench. On the field the Yankees execute. So many new faces, Sut thinks, looking down the bench. New rookies out on the field. Strangers, a new generation. Will any of them stick? The odds are so long against you ever making it, almost a random event. Not all the good ones make it, Bunyan said once. Not all the ones that make it are good.

Now that one over there. The papers are full of him. A bonus baby, the natural for third base says long chorus, big strong kid signed right out of high school. He could be the one, they say, a bull, a player to last forever, there are seasons yet to come in this game and he could be the one, the one to smash *all* the records, hit home runs a country mile and run and win ball games and pennants in the bright beckoning future, the game's greatest hero ever...

And some day, later, hero or not, he'll sit right here, look down the bench at the same different young faces, young confused or confident but unquestionably young, in the game running across the field he might slip once, stumble and recover before Ralph notices but the kids will see, when he ducks away from a rookie's wild pitch and the ball breaks sharply back across the plate, he'll think—but you never think in this game, just react, follow the bouncing leather ball, the very first thing you forget—

"McCaslin! Grab you a couple bats!"

Sut looks down the bench. Ralph motions to him. His hands jerk, his eyes wander in circles around the ballpark, he rises and sits again. Ralph has become an ancient in the dugout, senile and doddering, at the end of his baseball year. Every season he lives out the same cycle. Today is the last day. Sut looks at Keyser. Ed nods once, curtly.

There's a game on. The Yankees are beating the Senators.

Ralph points again. "You're up there, McCaslin." Sut grabs a couple of bats. The pitcher is due to bat in the last inning. They have stopped keeping score, the game is long over. Sut is the last batter. The loud-speakers boom—the stands echo quickly. Sut swings the bats over his head and drops one, marches to the plate.

The pitcher leans forward and stares at his catcher.

Sut waits.

The Yankee pitcher in pinstripes, the tall Georgia cracker, the mean city black, fat smiling farm kid, young Yankee pitcher leans back and reaches and rushes forward and—there was something Sut remembers, something Slade told him, was it maybe about this kid, was it something else or was it even dead Slade at all—on the mound the kid has all the moves, long flapping arms, twists and turns and releases a tiny message for Sut.

Printed in the United States
849200004B